LOST IN TIME

"You always told me the one thing you missed about Montana was teaching in a one-room schoolhouse instead of being nothing but a cog in a machine." She frowned. "A machine that threw you out as soon as you needed repair." The frown disappeared as she concentrated on folding another dress into my valise. "Conconully's an odd little place, but the people are friendly. It's where I grew up–" another little hesitation "–and I'd have stayed if I could, but there's no work for a journalist there." Her expression turned peculiar, then she turned back to my now-almost full valise, muttering, "except for one story, but nobody'd believe me."

"Jean, do they know about my, my–" now it was my turn to hesitate. I could not bring myself to say the words, do they know I am dying?

"Yes, they know you're ill. It's all right, Claudia." She looked up at me again, her eyes brimming. "Please, do this for me. It's all right."

And so it was that a little over two hours later, I found myself on a train headed east on the bridge over Lake Washington, away from my dearest friend, who had stuffed an assortment of tickets into my pocketbook and told the conductor to watch over me. She'd hugged me one last time and made me promise once again that I would use them all and follow her instructions to the letter.

I had promised I would. Heaven help me.

Books by M.M. Justus

Tales of the Unearthly Northwest

Sojourn

"New Year's Eve in Conconully"

Reunion

Time in Yellowstone

Repeating History

True Gold

"Homesick"

Finding Home

Much Ado in Montana

Cross-Country: Adventures Alone Across America and Back

REUNION

THE SECOND TALE OF THE UNEARTHLY NORTHWEST

M.M. JUSTUS

Carbon
River
Press

Reunion

First print edition published by 2015 Carbon River Press
Copyright © 2015 M.M. Justus
Cover art copyright © Can Stock Photo Inc. / johnnorth
and © Can Stock Photo Inc. / Anterovium
Cover design copyright © 2015 M.M. Justus
978-1522700494

Carbon River Press
http://carbonriverpress.com

ACKNOWLEDGEMENTS

Thank you again to the real towns of Conconully and Molson, Washington, and to the Okanogan County Historical Society.

And to my editor Elizabeth McCoy.

REUNION

CHAPTER 1

"Please, Miss Ogden, sit down." The principal's voice was kindly but sad, as was her smile, If I hadn't already known the news was going to be bad simply because I had been called into her office, it was as certain now as the pain. And that pain was a fact of life. Had been since before I'd taken this new job in Seattle, almost a year ago now. But it had worsened to the point that I'd missed days of classes, unable to rise from my bed. Too many days. Which was why I was here, now, sitting in Miss Taylor's office, waiting to be told they'd have to let me go.

"Have you seen a doctor?"

"Yes." I had finally, at Jean's insistence, used the money I owed her for rent and made an appointment, for all the good it had done me. Now I was in debt to her and no better off for it. Worse off, given what was about to happen to me.

"Was he able to discern what the problem is?" Perhaps she was hoping I'd tell her he was curing me. Maybe she wanted to keep me. If nothing else, it would save her the trouble of hiring someone else.

But no. Dr. Spencer had been useless to me, for all he'd tried to hide the fact. I'd seen it in his eyes. I swallowed. "I-it's female troubles, ma'am."

Her face grew grim. "You're not with child, are you?"

My breath left me in a whoosh of a "No!" But her expression did not change, and I could feel the hopelessness settling into my soul along with the pain that even now was making it difficult to keep my back straight and not bend me over. I shook my head, to add to the emphasis. If only that was the problem. But whatever trouble was in my womb, the doctor could not determine what it was, and could not do anything.

"Will you be well soon?"

I shrugged helplessly. "I don't know. The doctor doesn't know, either."

Her brow furrowed. "Will you be going to a specialist?"

Dr. Spencer had broached the subject, but I could not afford it, not on a teacher's salary. "No, ma'am."

Miss Taylor's expression faded into something resembling pity. I supposed I did seem pitiful to her, but I could not muster the dignity to deny it.

"You have missed six days in the last month, and more than two weeks since term began two months ago." She paused, as if she didn't want to do what I, or my illness, had forced her to do. "I am sorry, Miss Ogden."

I blinked my stinging eyes, determined not to shame myself in front of her. Not any more than I already had. "Yes, I know. I will gather my things."

I had reached the door and put my hand on the knob when she said, "You are one of the best teachers I've ever had the pleasure to work with. I wish you well, Miss Ogden."

At least I made it out of the building before the tears began to fall.

"That witch!" Jean exclaimed. "Why not kick you to the gutter as well as knocking you down?"

"It was not her fault." I sank into one of the two armchairs flanking the fireplace. The parlor of the little house in west Seattle I shared with my friend and landlady was a warm and cozy space.

Three steps took Jean across the room. She turned back to face me. "They have an obligation to help you, Claudia, not to make things worse."

I stared at her. I should have expected something like this from Jean, whose thoughts on the subject of employee/employer relations put her somewhere on the far side of the radical Wobblies. The Industrial Workers of the World had caused a general strike in Seattle a few years ago, and, from what I understood, had not accomplished a thing besides bringing the city to a standstill. But I had not expected it. I had expected her to take my side, and be sympathetic, and do all the normal things one's friends do when one stumbles over misfortune. But no. She had to make even my illness someone else's responsibility.

"The district cannot afford to keep a teacher who is too ill to teach."

"Then they should pay for the care that will make you well again. Your principal said you are the best teacher she's ever worked with."

I should not have told Jean that, but it was the one bright spot in this awful day. "One of the best, yes." I could not help smiling.

She did not smile back at me. "And yet she let you go because you are too ill to work. Have you made an appointment with that specialist yet?"

I did not reply, but she apparently saw my answer in my face, because her frown deepened into a scowl. "If you do not, I shall do it for you."

"Jean–"

But she rode right over me. "What was his name? Dr. Whittington?"

"Jean—"

But she was already on the telephone, speaking with the operator. While I wished I had the strength, or the determination, to stop her, I sank back in the chair in defeat.

She went with me, too. "To make sure you don't back out," she told me. Jean was a good friend. Bossy and overbearing and thoroughly convinced she always knew best, but a good friend. And when the appointment was over, and payment was mentioned, she glared me down and produced the cash herself.

It wasn't charity, I told myself. But it was. And I was so beaten down by what the specialist had told me I let her do it. She knew my situation from that alone, even though I'd been fighting to keep my despair from my face the moment I walked out of the examining room. The doctor had performed enough humiliating and, as it turned out, unnecessary scrutiny to tell me what my heart had already known before I left Montana last year. After all, wasn't that the main reason I'd left in the first place? Perhaps not the main reason, as I had wanted the adventure, and to relieve my parents of one more burden as well. After all, my intellect, such as it was, had refused to believe what my heart knew until I could ignore it no longer.

Jean did not say anything until we reached our house – her house, really, as I was simply her tenant as well as her friend, and would not be either, or anything, much longer – and the door closed behind us.

She waited, until I fell more than sat into that same wing chair where she'd bullied me into going to the appointment where I'd heard my sentence. Then she said, more gently than I'd ever heard her before, "That bad, is it?"

I nodded, tried to speak, couldn't, and she sank down on the arm of the chair, putting a warm arm around me. "I am so sorry, my dear."

She leaned away from me, as if ashamed of her kindness, and added in a tone more like herself, "What will you do now?"

Because of course I could not batten on her charity forever. "I don't know. Go home, I guess."

"You are home," she told me firmly.

It was kind of her, but no. "I meant Montana." Not that I could batten on my family, either. They could not afford to take me in, not with six other mouths to feed and my father's work tenuous at best.

"Is that what you want?"

Of course it wasn't, and she knew it. What I wanted was my job, my home here, my friends, Jean. My normal life. But it had been snatched from me by my incurable female troubles, by this – cancer, the specialist had called it – growing in my womb. He had offered surgery, to remove it, but said it had probably already grown to other parts of my body. If I had come in when I'd first felt the pain, I might have had a chance, but now... He'd trailed off, his expression almost accusatory, as if it were my own fault I'd gotten sick, that I hadn't had the money to come see him, let alone the time and money to let him cut into me–

"No, but I cannot stay here."

"No, you can't."

Well, that was clear and sharp enough. And cold. I jerked myself up out of the chair. "I will gather my things." I had no idea where I would find the money for the train ticket, but at least my parents would be more sympathetic than this. I had thought she was my friend, no, she *had* been my friend. I hadn't known she was going to turn so suddenly cruel.

"No!" Jean's hand came down on my arm. "That's not what I meant and you know it."

I could not help but stare at her. Her voice was choked, and her eyes brimming. "I do not wish you to leave. I wish more than anything that you could stay."

"I-I know." And oddly enough, I did believe her. Whatever her reason for wanting me gone, I knew it was not because she did not care.

Her brows came together. Her mouth set, and she straightened her shoulders. "I know where you can go. They'll help you there." As I continued to stare at her, speechless, she told me, in the tone I'd long since learned not to even try to gainsay, "And you *will* go. If I have to drag you there myself."

Well, and what else could I do? I could not fight both Jean and my pain. Nor the despair born from the hopeless diagnosis the doctor had given me. The three combined to put me to bed, where I lay curled like a homunculus, breathing through the throbbing ache in my womb, unable to think, or even wonder. I heard the front door thump closed as Jean left the house.

I must have slept completely through the night in spite of everything, because the shadows were at an early morning angle through my bedroom window when I woke. Jean was standing in the doorway, a satisfied look on her face. "They'll take you," she said. "I knew they would."

"Who?" I started to ask, but she had opened the door to my wardrobe.

"Where is your valise?"

"Under the bed. Jean—"

But she was already there. "Your train leaves in two hours."

I had stared at her before, but this was sheer disbelief. "My train where?"

She dragged my valise out, opened it, and started packing my things with the practice of long experience. As an aspiring Nellie Bly – not that she called herself that but it was what she was – she was used to packing her bags on a moment's notice. It was, she'd told me when she'd first invited me to live here, why she wanted a housemate: to watch over her things and have someone living in the house while she was gone.

She glanced up at me, grinning. "Conconully."

"Conco–" I stumbled over the unfamiliar name.

"Conconully. It's a tiny place, out in the middle of nowhere, but you grew up in Montana, so that shouldn't be a problem for you. They need a schoolteacher, and have for a long time–" she hesitated briefly "–and it should suit you right down to the ground."

Startled out of my, well, startlement, I asked, "How would you know that?"

"You always told me the one thing you missed about Montana was teaching in a one-room schoolhouse instead of being nothing but a cog in a machine." She frowned. "A machine that threw you out as soon as you needed repair." The frown disappeared as she concentrated on folding another dress into my valise. "Conconully's an odd little place, but the people are friendly. It's where I grew up–" another little hesitation "–and I'd have stayed if I could, but there's no work for a journalist there." Her expression turned peculiar, then she turned back to my now-almost full valise, muttering, "except for one story, but nobody'd believe me."

"Jean, do they know about my, my–" now it was my turn to hesitate. I could not bring myself to say the words, *do they know I am dying?*

"Yes, they know you're ill. It's all right, Claudia." She looked up at me again, her eyes brimming. "Please, do this for me. It's all right."

And so it was that a little over two hours later, I found myself on a train headed east on the bridge over Lake Washington, away from my dearest friend, who had stuffed an assortment of tickets into my pocketbook and told the conductor to watch over me. She'd hugged me one last time and made me promise once again that I would use them all and follow her instructions to the letter.

I had promised I would. Heaven help me.

CHAPTER 2

I almost felt as if I was going home, once the train crossed the pass to the east side of the mountains. The forest changed from firs and maples so dense with undergrowth that I could not see far beyond my window, to the pines scattered across parklike golden meadows the autumn rains already soaking Seattle would never touch. Snow fell gently over the pass but had not yet reached here, although when I touched the window, the glass was cold.

The conductor had taken one look at my ticket and said, "Just to Wenatchee, miss?"

All I had been able to do was nod. I had not had the chance, or the time, to look at the small stack of pasteboard slips wrapped in a piece of paper torn from one of the lined newsprint pads Jean used for her writing. Once I was settled into my seat, I was almost afraid to look at them, for fear I would be tempted to follow her instructions.

But, except for the bit of cash that had not so mysteriously appeared in my pocketbook, the tickets were the only currency I had. Reluctantly, I unfolded the paper, and read.

"Dear Claudia,

   I know you think I've lost my mind, and I half suspect you're already thinking about cashing the other tickets in and seeing how far the money can take you. Please don't. If the world in general, and your former employer in specific (who makes me want to be very unladylike and spit on her for telling you in one breath that you're the best teacher they've ever had and in the next that you're not worth what it would take to help you) are determined to make your life miserable, then I wish to do for you what you really deserve.

What did she think I deserved? To live? I still did not understand what she thought sending me away to this place would accomplish. Even if they gave me a job, I would not be able to keep it. And then where would I be?

   Can you trust me? Please? I know trust isn't something you're used to doing, but just this once?

It was not a matter of trust. I was dying, according to the specialist. Something evil was growing in my body, something uncurable. I did not wish to die alone in a strange place. But I could not go back to the little house in west Seattle. Jean had made that abundantly clear, and I had nowhere else I could go there. I could not go back to Montana. I had not even had the chance to tell my family about my misfortune, nor did I wish them to know. They could do nothing for me, and it would only upset them. I leaned back in my seat and stared out the window at the rolling sagebrush hills that had taken the place of the open pine meadows. The late autumn sun glinted low in the sky, almost hurting my eyes. What could I do?

   I read on.

When you get to Wenatchee, take one of the hansoms to the steamboat dock. The second ticket will get you aboard the Columbia Belle, and a berth where you can rest. The boat will arrive in Brewster in the morning. At Brewster, you'll need to get to the stagecoach station on the main street – Brewster is tiny, it's only a five-minute walk from the dock. The third ticket is for the stage to Omak.

Now it gets a bit odd. The morning after you arrive in Omak – I recommend the Wiggins Hotel, not that you'll have much choice in the matter, and get as much rest as you can – you'll need to go to the riverfront again, and find a teamster named Oscar Miller. He'll take you the last of the way to Conconully.

When you get to Conconully, ask for Max Pepper. Tell him Jean sent you. Everything will be all right. Take care, dear. I know you don't understand now, but you will. And perhaps I'll see you again someday. It is my fondest wish.

Jean

Yes, I was weary. And overwhelmed. And every rattle of the train hurt. And I still did not understand why Jean had done all this for me. Or why she had spent so much money to do it. It was hard to be grateful, as I supposed she thought I should be. But as she had said about the hotel in Omak, I did not have much choice in the matter. I would go to this town Conconully, and, if they would hire me after they saw how ill I really was, I would take the teaching job. I would earn a living at the one thing I loved more than anything for as long as providence allowed me to do it, and if nothing else, I could be of use to a town so isolated that they would take the likes of me as a teacher. Perhaps one of my students would go on to great things, and would remember my help. It was the only immortality I was likely to have.

The rest of my journey ran far more smoothly than I had expected. The hansom driver at the Wenatchee station took one look – and pity, I suspect – on me, and I arrived at the steamer dock with time to spare. The steward took equal care, and the cabin he led me to was far nicer than I had thought it would be. I sank onto the small but surprisingly comfortable bed in the tiny room it seemed I was to occupy all by myself. Utterly exhausted, I fell asleep before the sun sank below the mountains.

We arrived in Brewster the middle of the next morning, and again, people were far more helpful than I had any right to expect. I was on the stage out of town after a noon meal at a tiny shack the steward had recommended, that had tempted even my dulled appetite.

I wondered, as one gentleman assisted me onto the stage as a second put my valise in the boot, if I would regret the meal. The coach was dusty and rather battered-looking, and I suspected the road to Omak would be rough.

As all stagecoaches are. But I was still so weary, in spite of the sleep I'd had, that I do not remember much of the ride. I woke with a jerk when the stage stopped.

"Have a good nap?" The gentleman who had helped me to my seat smiled down from where he sat next to me, and I realized I had been resting my head on his shoulder.

"Oh!" I said, "I am sorry."

"Nothing to apologize for. You look a bit puny. Are you all right?"

I was not about to answer that question truthfully. "Yes, thank you. Where are we?"

"Omak."

"Already?" But I realized the light was fading outside and the air was nippy. Exactly how long had I slept? At any rate, I was glad for having done so. I was holding up better than I would have expected, in spite of everything.

"This where you get off?"

"Yes. Thank you." This as he rose to assist me down from the stage, and went to retrieve my valise.

"Thank you," I said again and reached to take it from him.

"Where're you headed?"

I shook my head to clear it. It did not help much. "I need to find somewhere to stay for the night."

"Goin' on from here in the morning?" I don't know what he saw in my face at his question, but his smile turned wry. "Sorry, miss. Woman travelin' alone might want a protector, but you don't know me from Adam, do you?" He shifted my valise to his other hand — where was his luggage? — and held his right hand out to me. "I'm Walt McMillan. Let me help you to your hotel, at least."

I took his hand. It was warm and firm and calloused. "Thank you." And then I remembered. "My friend recommended the Wiggins Hotel."

"Your friend's got good taste."

And so yet another kind stranger helped me find what turned out to be a pleasant establishment overlooking the river. I spent rather more of Jean's money for the room than I would have liked, but I felt safe there. In the event, I was in enough pain that evening so as to be of no use for finding another.

I suppose it was the ache that wearied me enough to put me to sleep. I woke early, feeling better, at least for the time being. After a breakfast I knew I needed but barely choked down, I bundled up against the cold and made my way carefully down the dusty main street running parallel to the river to the only dock I could see. It was perched on a bit of a point sticking out into the river, with two cargo steamers pulled up each to one side. A constant parade of men carried barrels on their backs or toted boxes and sacks. They traipsed up and down the dock and the dirt track leading up from it to a large warehouse, its wooden walls gray with weathering. A man in dirty worn overalls and a felt hat stood at its entrance, directing them.

I did not know who else to ask. The clerk at the hotel this morning had claimed no knowledge of anyone named Oscar Miller. Hesitantly, I approached the man.

I had to clear my throat twice before he noticed me, and then he only did so when one of the laborers jerked his head in my direction as he was taking his instructions.

"Yeh?" He sounded impatient, so I answered as quickly as I could.

"I'm looking for Mr. Oscar Miller, from Conconully. Do you know where I might find him?"

I had not been expecting the shocked stare he was aiming in my direction now. "What do you want with Miller?"

It really was none of his business. I repeated myself, wondering if something had happened to the poor man and if something had, then what would I do?

At last he shook his head. "Your funeral." He pointed to another building a bit further down the road.

Building was too kind a word. A pile of silvery gray worn planks leaned precariously as if in search of something sturdier to hold it up. I glanced back at the man, but he was already directing the next several laborers as to where to put their loads.

I shrugged, picked up my valise, and trudged toward it.

I hardly expected to see anyone working in such a place, but as I approached the ware– shack, I suppose I could call it, I saw a the rear end of a wagon sticking out from behind it, the back side of its box lowered to create a slope for loading. The wagon was almost full, mostly with barrels, but with boxes and crates and a few large sacks as well.

I stepped forward to get a better view, and saw eight mules – healthy, glossy-looking beasts, hitched and ready to go. Obviously prepared to pull a heavy load. Even as I admired the animals, a man appeared from behind the shack, rolling another barrel in front of him.

He was old. Not just the kind of old-before-his-time from doing manual labor all his life like my father, but too old for the work he was doing. The barrel was obviously full, and had to have weighed more than he did, but he pushed and strained and used a slat as a lever, and manhandled that barrel up the ramp onto the wagon. He straightened, leaning against it to keep it from rolling back down and rendering all of his effort moot, and put a hand to the small of his back.

I could see he was breathing hard. I could also tell the moment he saw me. He turned away, and with an equal effort, tipped the barrel up on end and nudged it to join its fellows. But in the instant before he did, I thought I saw his eyes widen.

I stepped forward. "Mr. Miller? Are you Mr. Oscar Miller?"

Any fear I had harbored that he would not acknowledge my existence was relieved when he turned back to look down at me. "Who wants to know?"

It was not exactly the kindness I had been surrounded with until this morning, but I forged on. "My name is Claudia Ogden. I was told you might be able to take me to Conconully."

He stared rudely at me for a long moment. At last he said, "I don't know what you're talking about."

He had to. Or he had to know who would. "You are not Mr. Miller? Do you know where I can find him? My friend Jean Clancy said he would be able to help me."

His eyes widened briefly again, but he shook his head, as if trying to decide whether giving me his name would cause more harm than good. "I'm Miller." I had the very strong impression he wished he could have said otherwise.

Relief washed over me. "Oh. I am so glad. Can you take me to Conconully? Miss Clancy said you would."

He shook his head again. "No, I can't." He looked me up and down. I knew my distress was written across my face. My troubles chose that moment to give me a particularly sharp throb of pain, and it was all I could do to keep my back straight. "Go back where you came from, city girl. You don't know what you're getting into out here."

If only I could. "I have nowhere else to go. I will pay you–" No. My pocketbook was almost empty. Had Jean known this lack would push me on when nothing else could? "I do not have the money yet, but as soon as I start working again I will."

An odd expression flitted across his face, but it vanished before I could make sense of it. I could not decipher it except to understand somehow that he *could* take me, and he would not tell me why he *would* not.

"Please, sir. I-I have nowhere else to go."

Now I did recognize the expression on his face. Pain of his own. "I can't help you, young lady," he said at last. "And I don't know of anyone alive who can."

After a few more moments of utter silence, he went for another barrel. I watched him load that one, then another, and when he stopped to catch his breath again, I took a deep one of my own. "Where are you going with this load?"

He sighed and finished loading the barrel. "I can see you won't believe me without the proof of your own eyes."

"Should I?" I asked him. "Would you?"

"Prob'ly not." He turned back to look at me again, one foot propped on a wheel spoke. After a moment he seemed to come to some conclusion.

I tried not to look as desperate as I felt. "What have you to lose?"

That startled a rusty chuckle out of him. "You've got a point, young lady. All right. I'm almost done here. But it's your funeral."

It was the second time I had been told so this morning. Before today I had not heard anyone use that expression since my grandfather, who had died when I was a child. I sincerely hoped Mr. Miller did not mean it literally. I was close enough to that state as it was.

CHAPTER 3

After he loaded the last barrel, Mr. Miller took my valise, tucked it underneath the backless, cushionless, wagon seat between the two barrels helping to hold it up, and assisted me onto the hard wooden bench. I was grateful to be off my feet, but I sincerely hoped Conconully was not far, as this was not much of an improvement and my endurance was at a low ebb.

He strolled around to the other side by way of his mules, stopping to pat and give a good word to each of his obviously well-tended animals.

If it were not for those mules, and those creatures no rational reason at all, I think I would have scrambled back down, even with nowhere else to go. If it were not for those mules, that is, and for Jean's insistence. And now, I was beginning to realize, for my own curiosity.

It was as if Jean had set me off on some sort of quest, and everyone I had come into contact with since I'd left Seattle had been told to help me on my way. Everyone except Mr. Miller, that is, and even he hadn't discouraged me so much as given me a reason to fight to get my way. I could no more have gone anywhere else now without finding out what all the mystery was about, than I could have flown over the mountains.

I watched the old teamster surreptitiously watching me as he finished checking his sturdy mules and climbed onto the seat next to me.

I put my handbag down between my feet, Mr. Miller picked up the reins, and, with a jolt, the wagon began to move.

We soon left the little town of Omak behind, climbing up the steep bluffs west of town on a road that began as a graveled street, dwindling down to a dirt lane and then to nothing more than two worn wheel tracks running through the grass. The mules took the climb in stride, pulling the wagon with an easy effort, encouraged by Mr. Miller's occasional comment and light hand on the reins.

The late autumn wind whipped down off of the snow-capped peaks to the west with a dry cold completely unlike the damp chill of Seattle. The tall grasses brushing the sides of the wagon were stiff with hoarfrost, sounding like brooms sweeping across a wooden floor as we moved along. But the sky was a brilliant clear blue, the air was crisp, and, even as I tucked the ends of my scarf more securely around my neck, and pulled my hood forward to cover my ears, I breathed in deeply.

The air tasted almost like home.

Please do not mistake me. I liked Seattle. It was the biggest city I had ever seen, lively and important and full of mischief and inspiration. And beautiful, surrounded by water and mountains, with the grand peak of Mount Rainier towering above everything on the southeast horizon when the weather was clear, which was seldom enough most of the year. But it lacked horizons. Unless one strolled onto the beach at Alki, or rode a Mosquito Fleet boat out onto the Sound, heading for one of the islands or the isolated towns across the water, it was difficult to see any distance for the hills and thick forests.

Here, as I turned and looked behind me when at last we reached the top of the bluff, I could see almost to Montana, or so it seemed. Down to the river, where the twin towns of Omak and Okanogan clung to the shore a mile or so apart, across the river to the black cliffs and the rolling landscape beyond.

"Goes on forever, don't it?" said my companion at last when I turned around, sounding as if now that he had given in, there was no point in being surly. "Sure that's not the direction you want to be headin'?"

Ahead of us lay the eastern foothills of the Cascade Mountains, a wide valley between rolling hills. Not quite as wide a horizon, but still crisp and clear, unlike the moisture-blurry air west of the mountains. Off in the distance, I saw animals, a good-sized herd. I pointed, and my companion chuckled.

"Elk. Not as many left these days. They weathered wolves and fire and everything else nature could throw at 'em, but men get greedy." He shrugged. "Can't blame 'em, I guess."

I was not sure if he wished to blame the men or the elk. "They are beautiful."

"They're critters." He fell silent again.

After a time, shifting uncomfortably on the hard board seat, I dared to ask, "How far is it to our destination?" Bringing up the name Conconully did not seem like a good idea, given his reaction to my first mention of it, but for all I knew we could be traveling for days. I was not prepared for sleeping out in the open, not to mention alone in the middle of nowhere except for someone I knew nothing about except his name and Jean's confidence. But she hadn't seen him for years. People did change.

He smiled down at me. He really was a rather large man, and I should have been frightened of him. I knew I should not be alone with him out here, on our way to a place he did not seem to want to admit even existed, but here I was. A sudden and inexplicable feeling of safety and warmth enveloped me.

Mr. Miller chuckled. "My wife would have liked you."

Taken aback, I said, "Would have?" and immediately regretted the question.

His face closed down and he made quite the affair of reaching into his pocket for a handkerchief and blowing his nose while hanging onto the reins. I would have offered to take them while he managed the business, but while the eight mules were still pacing along in perfect harmony, I had no illusions about being able to control them if that situation should change.

He did not answer me. He had not answered either of my questions, in point of fact.

"I am sorry for your loss," I said to the air in general, and listened to the grass sweeping the sides of the wagon as the only reply I received.

When the sun had reached far above the hills and beamed bright but unwarming light down upon us, Mr. Miller brought the mules to a stop near the creek we had been following for about an hour. "Need to rest and feed."

I assumed he meant the animals, but he also brought out a parcel tucked into the back of the wagon and handed it to me before he went to unhitch the team.

Surprised, I opened the parcel, and could feel my eyes widen. Inside the bundle was more than enough food for two, and such food! Fried chicken still crispy even though cold, creamy potato salad, and a jar of preserved peaches. And underneath these riches, protected by a stoneware plate, sat two large pieces of apple pie.

"Oh, my," was all I could think to say. My mouth was watering. The breakfast I had choked down at the hotel this morning seemed days ago. I had forgotten what appetite was like. It felt wonderful.

Mr. Miller looked up from where he was tending his mules and grinned. "Audrey's a good cook."

Was Audrey his wife? But no, that made no sense. I knew better than to ask. Once he climbed back up on the wagon seat, I spread the cloth our picnic had come wrapped in on the bench between us, and we both tucked in.

Impossibly, the food tasted even better than it looked. Between the two of us, we polished off every bit. I looked at my companion and said, without thinking, "If you eat like this every day, it surprises me you're not too heavy for the mules."

He burst out laughing, and I added, embarrassed, "It must be all the hard work." He nodded, still smiling, and I smiled back at him, feeling brave once more. "How much farther to our destination?"

He frowned, but not, it seemed, at me. "It's hard to tell."

How could he not know? I tried to think of a way to phrase it that would not cause him to close down again. "You must know how many miles it is from Omak to," I paused, still unwilling to risk saying the name, "our destination. And have at least a rough idea of how far we've traveled. Surely this isn't the first time you have made this trip."

He shook his head. At last he said, "I'm not so good with that kind of thing anymore."

An unease crept over me. "Surely you're not lost! You've been following the tracks..." I turned to stare back at the road we'd been following. Granted, it had become only two wheel tracks through the tall grass not long after we had left Omak, but those tracks had been distinct. Now, as I stared back the way we had come, I could see nothing. No wheel marks, no mule dung, not a single sign anyone had ever come this way, let alone a heavily-loaded wagon, eight mules, and two people.

Before I could turn back to him and ask all the questions boiling in my mind, Mr. Miller said, "Be right back. Got to–" he gestured.

He climbed down and disappeared behind some trees. I waited. What else could I do? He was simply answering a call of nature. I had done so myself earlier, catching up to the wagon as it rolled along slowly when I was finished.

But it was a long time before he finally came back, and when he did, his entire demeanor told me I would get no answers, quiz him as I might.

My uneasiness increased. I wished I had not given in to Jean's insistence. I wished I had never left Seattle. I wished I'd had somewhere else to go. But, as my mother used to say, if wishes were horses, then beggars could ride. I was here because it was the only option open to me. And, I had to admit, because Jean had been so convinced it would be the saving of me. It only went to show that she refused to believe the specialist, or thought I had not been honest when I told her what the specialist had said.

"Did you know my friend Jean?" I asked him. He now felt like a brick wall sitting beside me. "She grew up in Conconully." Silence. "I know you recognized her family name." Silence.

I took a deep breath. "Please, Mr. Miller. Perhaps you were right and I made a terrible mistake, asking you to take me to Conconully. Please talk to me. Tell me where we are and how much farther we have to go."

He suddenly straightened and relaxed. "Not much farther."

I sighed relief. Then we came around a bend in the creek and over a rise.

"Well," Mr. Miller said. "Here we are."

CHAPTER 4

"Here?" I croaked, and cleared my throat. "Where?"

Mr. Miller shrugged. "Conconully. What did you expect?"

"But–" I could say no more.

"You can't say I didn't warn you." He climbed down and went to the mules, taking the harness of the right lead animal and guiding it around in a circle so the wagon was facing the other way. Then he came to me, holding up his hands as if to help me down.

I did not move, to take them or to do anything else.

He shifted his feet. "This is as far as I go." The sadness was back in his eyes. No, not sadness, grief. Why, or who was he grieving?

"Where is the town?" I asked in bewilderment.

"Flood. Didn't you read about it? It was in all the papers when it happened." He lowered his arms and shrugged.

It didn't look like a flood had passed through here. It didn't look like anything had ever happened here. Only an open meadow, ringed with forest. "Why didn't you tell me?"

"Figgered you knew. Figgered your friend told you." He went around to the back of the wagon. I assumed he would come around to the other side and climb back on, take us on to wherever he was carting his load. Instead he began unloading, tilting and rolling the barrels as if they were much lighter than they had been when he'd first filled the wagon with them back in Omak. Or as if he was much stronger. The thought came to me unbidden and I shook it away as nonsensical. If anything, after a long day's ride, he should have been more tired. But his back was straighter and his arms were corded with muscle.

"What are you doing?" I asked, even though it was obvious.

He did not answer me. I climbed down and went to the back of the wagon. "Why are you unloading here?"

Wordlessly he pulled my valise from under the board bench and handed it to me, then spoke. "You wanted me to bring you to Conconully. You're here. My job's done." He looked as if he wanted to say something else, but thought better of it. Then he opened his mouth again as if he couldn't help himself. "Tell Rose– tell Rose I miss her."

I stared at him. "But no one is here!"

He did not answer me, but before long the wagon was empty and the barrels were neatly stacked on the rough meadow. He climbed back up onto the wagon seat. I tried to lift my valise, to put it back in the wagon, but a stab of pain hit me and I dropped it.

"You cannot leave me here!" Ignoring the sudden agony, I tried to scramble back aboard without my valise, but Mr. Miller shook the reins, and the mules began to move. I fell back before my foot was caught in the slowly spinning wheel spokes.

"Wait! Please!" I ran to follow it. "Don't leave me!"

The wagon, moving much faster now that it was empty, crested the rise and disappeared behind it before I could catch up. But when I reached the top myself, the wagon, the mules, and Mr. Miller were gone.

* * *

Not simply headed back where he had come from, but vanished, as if they had never been there in the first place. I sank to my knees in the tall grass and put my head in my hands. It was what I deserved for having gone off on this wild goose chase in the first place, I supposed. For listening to Jean in the first place.

But I'd had no one else to listen to, and nowhere else to go. She'd made it clear I shouldn't – couldn't – come back. I could understand that. Unemployed, ill, with no prospects, I would have been nothing but a weight on her and her resources. She'd owed me nothing, and yet she had, I thought, given me far more than I could have expected from her. She'd even said coming here would give me a prospect. But to do *this* to me?

Perhaps she hadn't known. Even as the thought passed through my mind, however, I dismissed it. She was a journalist. She not only followed the news, she reported on it, took it and made it her own. Yes, Conconully was – had been – a small town in the back of beyond, but it had been her hometown. She'd have read about the flood. She'd have known.

She'd sent me on a wild goose chase to nowhere. I wondered what she was thinking of me now, if she wondered if I'd caught onto her cruel joke. Send a dying woman to a dead town? Why? And spend her precious funds on my journey?

Now the only person who knew where I'd been abandoned was the man who'd left me here. The man who had utterly vanished, whose wagon and mules did not leave a trace of where they had passed.

I had no idea how to find my way back to Omak, let alone Seattle. And I had no one to blame but myself.

I lifted my head from my hands and stared at my surroundings, unseeing at first, then, though I'd have thought it wasn't possible to be more wounded and flummoxed than I already was, with an ever-growing sense of disbelief.

Nothing was right. Nothing made sense. Even the tiniest details were off.

It was late November. By rights my clothing should be wet with snow, and I starting to worry about frostbite. Instead I was almost too warm in my heavy woolens, hood, coat, scarf, and boots. I threw the hood back and let the sunshine beam its warmth down on my head – yes, the sky had been cloudless all day, but the sun had been so low as to feel like the perpetual sunset which was all winter ever gave us this far north. Now it was almost directly overhead, and I was perspiring.

I pulled off my gloves and unbuttoned my coat. After another moment, I took it off altogether and spread it over the grass to sit down and try to think what to do next.

The soft, supple, *green* grass of spring, not the dry brown broom bristles of winter. I glanced up to see enormous maple trees scattered across the meadow, their soft red-tinged green leaves beginning to accordion themselves open. Along the edge of the forest, shining new pale green needles on the larch trees glowed against the darker pines and firs.

It was as I was staring in wonder at this vision of spring in November that I first heard the voices. Not just one, but several, ranging from a deep male baritone to an unexpectedly authoritative-sounding soprano, all having what seemed from their tones to be a lighthearted conversation, although I could not make out the words.

I cannot explain how absolute the relief I felt was. I was not stranded here alone after all. I didn't know where the voices came from, or why these people were here. All that mattered was that I was not utterly abandoned, that I would survive, that they would help me.

Help me do what or go where, I had no idea, but at the moment that was completely beside the point.

"Hello?" I called eagerly.

The voices stopped. Not only the voices, but everything. Utter silence reigned around me. The bitter wind yanked at my scarf, and, no, I cannot explain it, but suddenly I was back in the middle of winter once more.

I could have wept, but it would do me no good. Braced against the ache in my abdomen, I stood and pulled my coat back on. The least I could do was go fetch my valise. Then I would find those people and ask, no, demand for them to help me.

As I made my way down the slope, the wind died down again, and suddenly I was back in spring. I could not hear the voices, although I vow I sensed, felt, *knew* I was not alone. I found my valise where I had left it. I picked it up with no trouble. Its weight was normal, even light, in my hand, not agonizingly heavy as it had been when I'd tried to put it in Mr. Miller's wagon.

The barrels were not as they had been when I left them behind. Not that I had paid them much attention at the time, but it had only been less than an hour, if that.

There'd been over two dozen barrels, all on end, all neatly stacked as if in a warehouse waiting for someone to come get them. Now, three of them lay on their sides, some little distance from the others, again in a tidy row.

I shook my head. Something was wrong, but it was not with my surroundings. This had to be some sort of dream. I must be still back in the little house in Seattle, in my bed, with Jean in hers in the next room breathing heavily in her sleep.

I *was* hearing breathing, but I was not dreaming. I was not in my bed in our– Jean's house in Seattle. I was out in the woods alone, far from anywhere with no hope of finding my way back.

"Please?" I called out desperately. "I know you're out there. I need your help."

A throat cleared behind me. I started violently and whirled around, dropping my valise with a thump.

A short, stout man in elegant clothing of the style of twenty years ago stood in front of me. He smiled at me in what I could not help but see as genial approval. "Hello, young lady. My name is Max Pepper. How may I be of assistance?"

I opened my mouth, but I could not find my voice. I swallowed and closed it again. It was as though he had appeared out of nowhere.

His expression changed to one of concern. "Are you ill? Let me fetch the doctor–"

I swallowed again. "No." No, I was not fine, but Jean had told me to find Max Pepper, and, glory be, I'd found him. I took a deep breath and let it out in relief "Where am I?"

He answered me with a question of his own. "How did you come to arrive here?"

Honesty was the best policy, especially with a potential employer. "Jean Clancy sent me. I came on the wagon that brought those barrels."

This gained me a completely unexpected reaction. His eyes went wide and he took a step back. And another. And another.

Before I could say anything to stop him, he was gone.

He was not gone long, however. Before I could think of what to do, whether to try to follow him or wait or panic, he had returned. And when he came back he was not alone. With him were a tall, angular, middle-aged woman; an older man judging by the color of his steel-gray hair; a tall young man with brown hair and a sheriff's star pinned to the chest pocket of his plaid shirt; and a short young blonde woman carrying a black leather bag and wearing men's *trousers*.

They all wore the same astonished expression, but, as I watched them, it changed to varying degrees of pleasure. Mr. Pepper looked positively smug as he observed his companions.

Before he could say anything, however, the sheriff stepped forward and held out his hand. Not knowing what else to do, I took it. His fingers were warm, even through my glove. He frowned, and turned to the blonde girl? woman? in her odd clothing. "Amy, she's freezing. We need to get her to town."

A strange lassitude had overtaken me at the touch of his hand. "I-I need to sit down," I told him, their figures wavering in front of me, and, I am ashamed to admit, I fainted dead onto the grass.

I do not believe I was "out," as the sheriff called it later, for long. When I awoke, I was riding between the older man and the sheriff, down the hill, in a sort of chair carry with their hands laced together underneath me and behind my back.

I struggled to get down, but the sheriff said, "It's all right. We won't drop you."

"I don't think that's what's worrying her, Dan," said the tall woman. She was right, of course, but only partly. I'd never felt so weak in my life, as if I hadn't slept or eaten for days.

"Please let me down," I asked, in spite of this.

I wished we'd been introduced properly, so I could demand it of them by name. The sheriff looked over at the blonde woman as if asking for permission.

"It would probably be better for her if you did," said the young woman. So they gently set me down on my feet. The older man held onto my arm. I suppose I looked as if I would fall over again at any instant, although I did feel a bit better now.

"Let go, Rob," the young woman said decisively. "She'll be stronger if you let her alone."

Scowling, the tall man did so. I swayed slightly, and he made as if to take hold of me again, but did not. And, oddly enough, I felt better standing on my own two feet, without support, which pleased me very much.

Mr. Pepper seemed pleased, too, and answered my unspoken wish, gesturing to each person in turn. "This is our sheriff, Dan Reilly, and our doctor, Amy Duvall, and Audrey and Rob Missel. And you are, Miss?"

Oh. The young woman was a *doctor*? I supposed that explained the black bag and the pulse-taking and all, but not the *trousers*. She certainly didn't look like any doctors of my acquaintance. Decidedly not like Dr. Spencer or the specialist. The more I considered that, however, the more it stood in Dr. Duvall's favor. "My name is Claudia Ogden."

"Well, then, Miss Ogden, if you're feeling up to it, why don't you come back to town with us?"

The relief was almost overwhelming. Town. There was a town. I had found Max Pepper and there was a town. "All right." I took one step, then another, and another, and before I knew it I was striding along with them on a dirt road that had appeared beneath our feet as if out of nowhere, alongside the chiming stream.

But something was missing– I stopped dead. "My valise! I need to go back and get my valise!"

"It's all right," Mr. Pepper told me. "The men have to go back and fetch the barrels. They'll bring your valise with them."

"My handbag!"

Mrs. Missel held out her hand. "I presume this belongs to you, then." I all but snatched the bag from her, then blushed, embarrassed at my rudeness.

She smiled at me. "It's all right. You've been through the bit of a shock, and there's more to come. We're very glad to meet you."

"Thank you." I paused, making the connection. "Are you the fine cook whose delicious fried chicken I ate on my way here?"

She positively beamed at me. "Why, yes, I am."

I did not begin to know what I should ask next. But no one had answered the most important question I had, and it came out more plaintively than I had intended. "Then perhaps you can tell me, please, where on earth we *are*?"

They were all smiling at me now. I wished I knew why. But as we rounded a bend and came over a slight rise in the road, the valley opened out, and in front of us sat what must have once been a prosperous town.

Prosperous no more, however. Nothing remained but tumbledown ruins scattered across the valley in a peculiarly orderly fashion, along what must have been a grid of streets but was now nothing but ruts in the green grass. Silvery wood lay strewn hither and yon, glass shards of broken windows glinting in the bright spring sunshine.

I stared at it, then at my companions. Two of them, Sheriff Reilly and Dr. Duvall, gazed back at me in what I can only call commiseration. The other three seemed not to notice my astonishment, although Mr. Pepper's smugness had not disappeared.

What has he to be smug about? I wondered wildly. Jean, what have you gotten me into?

As I gaped down at what I could only call a ghost town, Mr. Pepper swept his arm grandly at it, a strangely proprietary gesture. "Welcome to Conconully," he said proudly.

CHAPTER 5

The sheriff snorted, bringing me back to earth, after a fashion. "Doesn't look like much, does it?" he said.

"It's– it's *deserted*," I said desperately. These people were crazy. They had to be. Or else Jean had plunged me into some sort of nightmare, and I could not believe that.

"No, it isn't," Dr. Duvall told me, stepping closer and putting her hand on my arm. She pushed my sleeve up slightly to bare the skin of my wrist. I tried to pull away, but she said, "Just a moment. I want to take your pulse."

My pulse? The insubstantial weight of her fingers made me feel lightheaded, but I bore her hand on my wrist until she let go, nodding decisively.

"You've got a sturdy constitution, Miss Ogden, to take a shock like this in stride." She looked pleased. "Better than Sheriff Reilly here did, anyway."

She grinned as the sheriff spluttered. "I'd just been in a car wreck, with a concussion and a broken arm!"

I was almost distracted by this odd statement, but stuck to my guns. "Where am I, truly? Mr. Pepper?" I turned to look at the little man.

"My friend Jean said you would—" Would what? She had simply told me everything would be all right. I had believed her then because I'd had no choice. But everything was patently *not* all right, and what was I to do now? "She said to tell you she sent me," I ended rather desperately.

Amazingly enough, there was a great deal of throat clearing and gazing anywhere but at me. At last Dr. Duvall said brightly, "Well, that explains a lot. Not enough, mind you, but a lot."

Mrs. Missel said, "Hush, child."

"It's all right, Amy," Mr. Pepper said. "Oscar brought her."

The silence this time was shocked all around.

At last Mr. Missel said, "He said he couldn't. He tried."

Then Sheriff Reilly said, "You told *me* he was dead, Max."

Now it was Mr. Pepper's turn to glance away. We had almost reached the first tumbledown building on the edge of town by now. Dr. Duvall said, "I'll take her in until we figure out what to do."

Mrs. Missel said, "You've got a lot on your plate right now, what with the wedding and all." Nods all around. I thought I heard Sheriff Reilly say something under his breath, and Dr. Duvall glared at him, but Mrs. Missel overrode him. "Belinda was still looking for a boarder, last I heard. Let's see if she still is before you take on any more responsibilities."

Responsibilities? Well, I supposed I was a responsibility to them, especially after I fainted on them. It did not mean I had to like it. And it did *not* mean Jean hadn't been out of her mind to send me here. For a position? What position? I said, "Perhaps I should be on my way back to Omak." And from there to where?

"That would take some time to arrange," Mrs. Missel told me, much to my consternation. I started to speak, but she rode right over me. "That's Rob and Max's bailiwick. In the meantime, I'll go check with Belinda."

Dr. Duvall said, "She can come to my house for now, anyway. Unless you were planning to leave her standing in the middle of the street until you get back."

"She," I said, trying not to sound desperate, "would very much like to have a say in what is happening to her."

The sheriff laughed. "People tend to be kind of high-handed here. You'll get used to it."

"You need to sit down and rest, at least, Miss Ogden," Dr. Duvall told me firmly.

Mrs. Missel nodded. "That's a good idea. I'll bring supper over, so you needn't worry about that."

"So she won't have to eat my cooking, you mean." The doctor sighed, but she seemed more amused than anything else. "Thank you, Audrey."

Sheriff Reilly said, "Consider yourself lucky, Miss Ogden," and Dr. Duvall glared at him. He added, to her rather than to me, "You don't want her to get food poisoning."

Mr. Pepper said quickly, "If you two are still planning on getting married, you'd better learn when to hold your tongue, Daniel. Go on, Doc Amy. It probably wouldn't be a bad idea for you to keep an eye on Miss Ogden's condition for the nonce."

Dr. Duvall nodded. "If you'd come with me, Miss Ogden." She gestured toward the dilapidated building, which, I noticed, did have a door and an intact front window. She smiled at me, which I supposed was meant to be reassuring. "It's in much better shape on the inside than the outside."

"I certainly hope so," I muttered. I followed her as she strode through the knee-high grass and bits of detritus as if they weren't there. If I had not been watching her so carefully, I would not have caught her querying glance back at Mr. Pepper, nor his reassuring smile at her.

But she looked relieved as she turned the knob and pushed the door open. It glided on its hinges as if they were freshly oiled.

"Welcome to my humble abode," she said.

I glanced back at the others, who had already moved on. I knew, or had been told, at least, where Mrs. Missel was headed, but– "Where are the rest of them going?"

"To tell everyone else about you, I imagine." Obviously taking pity on me, she explained, "We don't get many visitors here. Come on. You're welcome to my spare bedroom until Audrey gets you settled. Which she will do. If Belinda can't take you, she'll find someone who can." She gestured me in, and, clutching my handbag, I stepped through the doorway.

"I don't want to be any trouble–" But I could say no more.

The young doctor was quite right. The tumbledown building *was* much nicer on the inside than on the outside. Unbelievably so. Her parlor was bright with large mullioned windows on two of the creamy white walls. Rag rugs covered the shining wood floors. A black woodstove with polished nickel trim took up one corner, with a chesterfield upholstered in a cheerful plaid and a wing chair arranged comfortably near it. The rest of the walls were lined with bookcases, and those bookcases were crammed with books.

"I'm sort of the ad hoc town library," Dr. Duvall informed me. "One of these days I hope we'll have a real library, but for that we'd need a real librarian, or at least someone who knows what she's doing."

She watched me as, distracted from the unreality of it all, I was drawn to the strange but colorful covers on the shelf nearest to me. An encyclopedia, twenty years out of date, and not one but several dictionaries. Darwin's *Origin of Species*. A large book called *Cosmos* by someone I had never heard of named Sagan, and shelves of books on geography, history, and gardening, among many other varied subjects.

What looked like hundreds of novels with author names on the spines I did not recognize as well as some I did. Dickens, Twain, yes, but Bujold, Peters, A-aaron-ovitch? Nothing in any sort of order. My fingers itched. Not only to organize them, but to read them. Every single one.

Dr. Duvall's next question reminded me of my manners, however. "What do you do for a living, Miss Ogden?"

Reluctantly I pulled myself away from all those enticing volumes. "I'm sorry. I teach school. Or I did."

"Really?" She sounded inordinately pleased. "Our last teacher left some time ago, and we haven't had one since."

I stared at her. "There are *children* living here?"

"Oh, yes. At least two dozen, probably closer to three. The schoolhouse is only one room, but the building's in fair condition. We've been hoping– You said you did teach. Not any more?"

I should have been honest with her right then, but the words simply wouldn't come. Like a coward, I changed the subject. "Who teaches them?"

"No one for some time, I'm afraid, except for what they learn at home." She smiled sadly. "I know you're exhausted. Come to my spare bedroom and lie down. Audrey will be along with supper soon."

I would have preferred to spend more time with the books, but she was gesturing me through an open archway and down a short hall.

"On the right," she directed me.

I opened the door and stopped, entranced again. "It's lovely." And it was. A large window with calico curtains graced the bright white walls. An iron bedstead painted spring green was made up with a thick feather bed and a vividly-colored log cabin quilt, and piled with equally plump pillows. On the wall opposite the bed was a dainty wooden kneehole dresser. A wardrobe in the same simple style stood in one corner.

"I'm glad you like it."

"Do you quilt?" I asked, stepping across the room to admire the workmanship on the coverlet, which was very fine.

"I don't, but a number of the ladies in town do," she said. "That was given to me in payment for services rendered." She cleared her throat. "I'm the town's only doctor, you see."

"You don't look old enough to be a doctor. And a lady doctor at that!"

I put my hand to my lips, but the young woman was laughing. "Tell me about it. I shocked the stripes off this staid old place when I first arrived." I started to speak but before I could ask her when she'd arrived and why she'd stayed, why she wore men's clothing and the other dozens of questions boiling in my mind, she changed the subject. "You do need to rest. You've had quite a day."

I *was* tired. But I was too keyed up to rest. I was about to say so when a knock sounded on the front door.

"That'll be your valise," Dr. Duvall said, sounding relieved. "I'll go get it." She glanced back at me as she headed out of the room. "Doctor's orders, Miss Ogden. You have to be exhausted."

She returned a few moments later with my valise. "I have to go out for a bit now. Once you've rested for a while, feel free to poke through the books. But please don't leave the house until I get back."

She'd been so kind to me, the least I could do was allow her my first name. "Call me Claudia, please. Where are you going?"

Her cheerful expression turned wry. "Claudia, then. Call me Amy. I'll be back soon, I promise."

And with that, she was gone.

I sat down on the bed, suddenly as exhausted as the young doctor claimed I must be. My valise sat on the dresser, looking no worse than I felt: dusty and travel-worn. At least I had my possessions, such as they were. I could not let my guard down, much as I wanted to.

I don't know why I felt that way. Things had happened exactly as Jean had told me they would. Well, perhaps not exactly as she'd said, but the essentials were there. I'd found my way to Conconully, and it appeared they were in need of a teacher here. I still wasn't sure why Jean had told me to make contact with Mr. Pepper. He'd more watched the rest of us like some kind of benevolent grandfather – not like mine, who had never had the leisure to be benevolent – rather than being helpful at all.

From what Amy had said, I suspected they would be glad to have me teach their school, for as long as I kept my illness hidden. Gingerly I felt my abdomen, but for once it did not send out tentacles of pain. It was a most pleasant absence of sensation, one I had not felt in some time. I knew better than to build any hope upon it, but I would take advantage of it while I could.

Suddenly I was not as exhausted as I should have been. I stood up and, surprising myself, did not head for the ad hoc library. It would be there when I had time for it. I knew it wasn't the polite thing to do, but I decided to explore the rest of this odd but very comfortable little house.

The hallway led past another bedroom, obviously that of my hostess, who, I noted as I peeked in, was not the tidiest person of my acquaintance. Clothes were strewn across the room, on the bed, on the comfortable-looking chair in the corner, on the floor. Both men's and women's clothing, I noted with surprise, and some of the men's clothing was far too large for Amy.

Max had mentioned something about a forthcoming marriage between her and the sheriff. Surely they were not anticipating– and if they were it was none of my business. I could only hope they would refrain from such carryings-on while I was staying in her home.

The next room was small, and filled with a large tub and a small set of shelves containing bathing utensils. A pump stood in the corner next to a rather odd-looking chamber pot, no, a commode, and a small sink. How convenient, I thought. Compared to the arrangements in the house I shared with Jean, it was quite modern-looking. Compared to everything else I'd seen here so far, it was another mystery.

The last room at the back of the house was the kitchen. Another wood stove, a second pump, and all the other accoutrements for preparing food. Dirty dishes sat in the sink, and papers and other detritus were scattered across every level surface. A door in the far wall had a window mounted in it. I went to look out.

An enormous back garden was just coming into its full growth. Various vegetables and flowers, lush and green, grew in well-tended order, a far cry from the untidiness indoors. I could not resist. Amy had told me I mustn't leave the house until she came back, but surely she did not mean I could not enjoy her garden.

Once I stepped outside, it became obvious the garden was shared. It was much bigger than it looked from indoors, and several of the rundown buildings – people's homes? – surrounded it. More than half of it was devoted to vegetables and herbs. I stooped to pick a sprig of mint, its bed bounded, quite practically, by a thick mortared stone edging to keep it from taking over the world, and sniffed its sharp sweetness as I rubbed a leaf between my fingers.

Rows of trees in full bloom caught my eye, and I could not help but wander closer. Fruit trees. I did not know enough to tell apple from peach from pear, but the scent of the blossoms was entrancing.

I could no longer see Amy's house behind me, and shrugged back a slight feeling of guilt at disobeying her instructions. The communal garden, hidden from my first view of the town by the enormous maple trees lining the dirt track as much as by the derelict buildings, had me thoroughly enchanted.

As I wandered on, I began to hear a sound like the humming of bees. I ignored it, having discovered a section of the garden devoted entirely to flowers, many of which were just coming into their first full flush of bloom. I had never seen such color grouped in one place before. I recognized yellow roses and purple flags and mats of tiny, clove-scented pinks among the dozens of unfamiliar blossoms.

The flowers seemed to be concentrated behind one of the buildings, with streaks of blue paint peeling off of its silvery planks. As I rounded it, reveling in the sights and scents and textures, the humming sound increased until it no longer sounded like bees, but like a cacophony of human voices.

They seemed to be emanating from the biggest building by far, and the one in the best repair, which was not saying much. Its roof was in reasonable shape, all of its walls were still vertical, and even its paint was intact, appearing as if it had been applied more recently than I would have expected.

In for a penny, as the saying goes. I strolled closer to the back of the building, leaving the lovely garden behind, passing through a small grove of pale green larch trees not much taller than I was.

The voices became louder still, and I began to be able to distinguish words.

"Where?"

"Time?"

"How?"

And a complete sentence, uttered, if I was not mistaken, by the sheriff. "This changes everything, people."

Utter silence. I stepped closer, and slipped through the door.

A throat cleared, and Mr. Pepper spoke. "That was the intent, was it not? Why we brought you here, Daniel, and Doctor Amy?"

"Oh, is that why, Max?" That was clearly Dr. Duvall's voice. "You never really bothered to explain the why to us. Or the how, for that matter."

"I don't know the how." Mr. Pepper sounded positively hangdog, as if somehow it was his responsibility and he had fallen down on the job. "Oscar managed this one on his own."

A sharp female cry, in a voice I did not recognize as either Mrs. Missel's or Dr. Duvall's. It sounded old, and in distress.

"Rose!" The outcry went up from several voices.

"Max, you idiot!" from Amy.

"Let her through," from the sheriff. A great shuffling noise, and two sets of rather determined-sounding footsteps.

"She's fainted." That was the doctor again, sounding disgusted.

Without realizing it, I had crept down the hall, toward the voices, to another doorway. The door was ajar, and I could not help myself. I peered in to see what was happening.

The enormous, dusty room was empty.

CHAPTER 6

"Uh-oh." This voice, that of a child and completely unfamiliar to me, floated out of the echoing room in the most guilty-sounding tones I think I had ever heard, which for a teacher is saying a fair amount. "Doc Amy?"

I stared in. Surely they were there, and I simply couldn't see them in the dark. Although why a crowd should meet in the pitch black was beyond me. But now I couldn't hear a thing. Not even the sound of breathing, except for my own.

At last I did hear one inhalation, deep and long and lung-bursting. And a voice. "Miss Ogden, I must ask you to leave now. Please go back to Dr. Duvall's house and wait there."

Mr. Pepper. And his voice was so full of authority I nearly did exactly as he asked, no, ordered. That had not been a request, but a demand.

I drew a deep breath of my own along with all of the courage I possessed. "No." It came out in my best teacherly "It does not matter who started it – all of you *behave*" tone of voice.

The collective gasp I heard then had to have come from at least a hundred sets of lungs. But still no one spoke. Until at last Mr. Pepper said, "Very well. Then I must ask you to close your eyes for a moment. I will tell you when you can open them again."

I wondered for a second what he would do if I said no to that. Then I thought, what can he do in a moment? "All right," I told him. "They're closed."

"I see." Utter silence again. The moment seemed to drag on forever. Then a sudden brightness beamed against my closed lids. If Mr. Pepper, suddenly much closer to me than he had been, hadn't chosen to say, "All right, you can open them now," I would have in spite of him.

I did so. And what I saw made *me* gasp, as if at a spasm of pain.

The room was now brightly lit with dozens of old-fashioned gas lights, stretching what had to be a hundred feet from end to end and more than half that distance from side to side, with a ceiling so far overhead the gas lights cast it into shadows. I could see the shining wooden walls, though, if not the floor. I could not see that floor for the people crowding the room. Well over a hundred, probably many more. All ages, both sexes. All staring at me, still in silence, although at least now I could hear their breathing. The stillness felt like shock, and I knew exactly how they felt.

I could not help reaching for the door jamb. It was definitely not my illness, but my legs did not feel as if they would hold me up on their own.

A throat cleared, and I turned to follow the sound. Mr. Pepper stood on a stage to my right, almost within arm's reach, in front of a huge red velvet curtain. He smiled down at me, but the expression did not reach his eyes. Was he worried? About what? "What do you see, Miss Ogden?"

I opened my mouth, could not find my teacher's voice, or indeed any voice at all, and swallowed.

"It's all right, whatever you tell me," Mr. Pepper added, in a coaxing tone.

"She's white as a sheet," said the sheriff, who had approached me through the crowd without my noticing. "Here. Sit down." He nudged me into a wooden chair, one of many around the edge of the room, and I, perforce, sat.

And found my voice at last. "Who-who are you? Where did all of you come from?"

The sheriff gave me a wry smile, looked up at Mr. Pepper, received a nod of, was that approval? and said, "*Now* you're welcome to Conconully."

The ensuing cacophony was louder than any classroom I'd ever been in. Nothing was explained to me. My hand was wrung until I found myself apologizing for not offering it because it was sore. I was the recipient of smiles ranging from shy to the enormous grin of one ten-year-old boy among the several dozen children in the crowd. Amy had been right about that – and why would she have been wrong?

I was introduced as "Miss Claudia Ogden. She's a schoolteacher," over and over, by both Mr. Pepper and Amy, who finally cut the unusual celebration short.

I still wasn't sure what they'd been celebrating. It wasn't as if they'd put out some sort of call for a schoolteacher and I had arrived to fill the position. Or at least no one mentioned Jean, and her efforts to send me here. Not even Mr. Pepper, whom Jean had supposedly contacted—no. She'd never said she'd contacted anyone here, only that they would welcome me. That was certainly true.

I'd never felt so welcomed in my life.

Another woman approached me, her eyes kind, her very presence something like a calm in the storm. She smiled at me. "It's become rather boisterous tonight," she told me. "But they mean well."

She was shorter than I, but taller than the diminutive Amy. Silver strands glinted in the gaslight, seeming to accent her otherwise dark hair. It was pulled into a braided knot at the back of her head, in an arrangement that almost seemed too old for her unlined face. Like most of the other people here, she was dressed in styles a decade or so out of date, but obviously well-made. Hers was a striped brown silk that gleamed like her hair in the gaslight.

She held out a hand, and I took it. Her palm was warm and dry and somehow comforting. "My name is Belinda Houseman. I am looking for a boarder, and I understand you're looking for a new home. I hope we might suit."

"I-I–" But I got no further before Amy came up next to me.

"Oh, good. Why don't you take her on with you, Belinda? I'll get Dan to bring her valise around."

"Amy." Miss Houseman's voice was soft, but it stopped the young doctor in her tracks. "Why don't you let her decide for herself." She turned back to me, still holding my hand. "Would that suit you, Miss Ogden?"

It seemed as good an idea as any. Better than I should have expected. But apparently I'd hesitated too long, because Miss Houseman said, "It would only be the two of us. Perhaps you'd like to come look at it first?"

That decided me. "No." And quickly, before she could change her mind about me, or worse, Amy could put her oar in again, I added, "I'm sure it will suit me beautifully."

I glanced over at Amy and caught her closing her mouth. She grinned at me.

"But I don't want to put Mr. Reilly to the trouble. I'll come get it myself."

"It's no trouble," the man himself answered. "You go on."

What could I say? I was tired and worn from my long day, Miss Houseman was gesturing encouragingly, and the sheriff and Amy had already vanished into the crowd.

As I followed Miss Houseman, I said, "I don't want to take the sheriff from the gathering. If you'd wait for me."

She smiled, an mischievous expression in her eyes. "I'll come with you. I suspect it may take the lovebirds longer than they anticipate to return, and you'll want to be settled in before you–" she hesitated.

"Before I collapse in a heap? Yes."

She gave me a concerned look. "Are you feeling faint again?"

Who'd told her about my embarrassing lapse in the forest? This is a small town, I reminded myself. Word had probably spread before I'd come to.

Dusk had already fallen and the first stars were twinkling. I followed her out the back door and across the gardens again, picking my way carefully. "Who takes care of all this?"

"You won't remember Cassandra in the hubbub back at the meeting hall. She's a quiet little thing. But when it comes to the fields, she's a bit of a martinet."

"Surely one person can't manage all of this."

"Oh, no. We all pitch in when she needs extra hands. We grow our own fresh produce here." So far out in the back of beyond they would have to. I suppose I had simply assumed a man would be in charge.

"They're beautiful. Not what I expected at all." I glanced back at Miss Houseman as we approached Amy's house.

The back door was still unlocked. I had thought to slip in and out without waiting for the little doctor and her beau, but sounds from the parlor brought me to a halt.

I had not meant to eavesdrop. I could not help it in fact, but their first few words had everything to do with the sheriff's feelings for

Amy and nothing to do with what I still didn't understand about where I was and who these people were. And then the voices stopped altogether and what sounded unmistakably like gestures of affection began. My face heating, I averted my gaze, tiptoed around the corner, and crept down the hall to Amy's spare room to fetch my valise.

But when I stepped from the hall to the parlor, a throat cleared. "Let me take that for you, Miss Ogden," said the sheriff.

I kept my eyes averted. "I can manage it, thank you. Miss Houseman is out back. I mustn't keep her waiting."

The valise was tugged from my hand. "Come on."

I looked up at him. He was grinning, with no signs of embarrassment whatsoever. I felt my face redden further.

He turned to Amy. "I'll be back in a bit, if that's okay."

"Sure." She was smiling, too, if a bit more self-consciously.

Miss Houseman did not look at all surprised when the sheriff followed me out the back door. In fact, she looked pleased with him, and told him so. In a manner of speaking. What she actually said was, "It does look like the manners we've been trying to teach you are finally beginning to take." Then she added, turning to me, "You'd have thought he'd been raised by wolves when he first arrived."

"Hey!" the sheriff said, but there was no heat in his tone. He smiled down at me and strode on. Miss Houseman and I followed.

I must admit I was weaving on my feet by the time we reached Miss Houseman's home, which was a larger domicile than I had expected, and not so derelict in appearance as I had feared, given what I had seen till now. Sheriff Reilly bade us good-night at her front door, and headed off back in the direction of the little doctor's house.

"It was good of him to take the time to come with us," I said.

"He's learning," was all Miss Houseman said, but I could hear the smile in her voice. She opened the door, gesturing me inside. I caught only glimpses of the dark rooms on the ground floor before she led me up a staircase, where she opened a door on the landing. "This is the room. I hope it will suit."

I could not see much until she lit the lamp sitting on a small table next to the bed, and not much more even then. Shadows delineated the usual furnishings, and starlight glimmered through a large window.

"It looks fine." My voice sounded weak and tired, even to me. Well, and the specialist in Seattle had warned me against overexertion, which had been unavoidable until this moment. As if reminded, I felt the familiar, stabbing ache. Surely it had been there all along, and I had simply been distracted from it with everything that had happened to me today.

Miss Houseman must have heard the exhaustion and uncertainty in my tone, because she said, "You'll be better able to tell in the morning. There's water in the pitcher, and fresh towels and soap. Is there anything else you need right now?"

I sighed. "Just the bed, thank you."

"Then I will take my leave. Rest as long as you need to. There'll be no hurry in the morning."

She let herself out, and it was all I could do to undress myself before I fell into the bed as if off of a cliff.

CHAPTER 7

I woke next morning to a room full of sun and birdsong. Opening my eyes, I gazed around at a very pleasant room indeed. The bed, I now had reason to notice, was soft and comfortable with a feather mattress and pillows. They rested on a painted iron frame like the one in the little doctor's spare room, this one dark blue. The chest and dresser and the rest were golden maple, simple and warm. The walls were painted a shade of blue much paler than the bedframe, and the mullioned window was dressed with lace curtains. Beyond the glass stood a pair of pale green larches, making everchanging patterns in the sunlight and breeze. All in all, bright and cheerful. I thought about my room at Jean's house in Seattle, and for the first time did not feel hurtful regret.

I sat up gingerly, but felt no physical pain, either. So perhaps I had not been simply distracted yesterday. I knew better than to think the lack meant anything but a temporary respite, but I would not despise such a gift, either.

I washed and dressed quickly. I supposed I should unpack my valise, but that could wait. I was eager to see the rest of my new surroundings.

I made my way down the stairs, through a cozy parlor, following my nose to the kitchen at the back of the house, where the smell of coffee wafted. Very strong coffee, if my nose was any judge, and perhaps slightly overbrewed, if I wished to be kind about it.

I found the cook at the stove, cooking a batch of scrambled eggs.

"I thought I heard you stirring," Miss Houseman said, and dumped what looked like more than enough pepper for a dozen eggs into the pan, which held perhaps five. "Would you like some breakfast?"

I did not think I would care for those eggs. "Just some bread and butter, I think, if you have any," I said, trying to be tactful.

"Oh, but you need to build up your strength." She dished up the eggs onto two plates and handed one to me.

It could not be helped. I took one bite of those eggs and my eyes watered. The coffee was no better. I added cream and sugar, which diluted the burned taste only slightly.

I chewed and swallowed and drank, wondering if my taste buds would survive. Perhaps, I thought a bit desperately, it would burn the tumor out of me.

"Do you–" I coughed. "Do you have any bread and butter?"

She did. Good bread, and fresh butter, too. And by the time I had downed a slice, with the cold milk she also brought to the table, I was able to breathe again. "Thank you."

"It's been some time since I've cooked for anyone else. I'm glad you enjoyed it."

I bit my tongue rather than tell her the truth. But if I was to board here, I thought ruefully, I would have to find some way to do the cooking myself without hurting her feelings.

After breakfast, Belinda showed me around her home. The house, being her workshop as well as her residence, was much more spacious than I'd have expected for a woman living alone. I was especially fascinated with her workroom, its walls lined with shelves loaded with bolts of fabric in many colors and patterns. In the middle of the room stood a huge table at a low height that looked odd until Belinda moved next to it and I realized it had been designed just for her. Next to it stood not one but two sturdy treadle sewing machines of different types. In a corner was another, smaller table, scattered with paperwork, and a chair. Open cabinets full of notions and tools took up what little space was left.

"I had no idea," I told her. "You are a businesswoman as well as an artist, Miss Houseman."

She blushed. I had not seen her do so before. "It is how I earn my living. Rob – Mr. Missel – helped me set things up originally, and built the shelves and table. I paid him in trousers. He's very hard on his clothing." She added, almost as an afterthought, "you know, as you are to be my boarder, please call me Belinda."

So we had come to terms without my knowledge? And the familiarity, so soon? I could not help but respond in kind. "Then you must call me Claudia."

She smiled at that, looking pleased. Then she startled me even more by taking my hand again, as she had last night. She led me back out of her workroom and across the parlor. "You, too, are a professional woman, and need a place of your own. Rob set up an office for me as well, but I haven't been using it. I find it more convenient to keep my business and my work close together. But I thought it might suit you." She opened a door I had not noticed earlier, and, letting go of my hand, gestured me in ahead of her.

I stepped inside. "Oh," I said, and could say no more. The room was as bright, open, and airy as the bedroom I'd slept in. A large cupboard stood in one corner. Two large uncurtained windows were positioned opposite one another in the far corner. One framed a view out into a group of leafing maples, and the other opened onto the same spring green larches I'd seen from my bedroom. Under it stood a large rolltop desk, open to display cubbyholes and drawers. The piece was fit for a principal, let alone for a lowly teacher. In fact, it was a nicer desk than the one in Miss Taylor's office back in Seattle.

"We can have Rob, if he has time, or Adam Willis move a bookcase in for you," Belinda said from behind me. "I'm sure you'll be needing one."

Moisture filled my eyes, and I raised my hands to my face to hide it.

She stepped forward. I could feel the tears rolling down my cheeks, but I could not stop them.

"Dear, I'm sorry. Is something wrong?" She pulled a handkerchief out of her pocket and handed it to me, waited patiently while I turned away in embarrassment and mopped the tears away.

"No," I managed, but she put her arm about my shoulders and led me back out, closing the door behind us.

"I am sorry," she said again. "I only thought you might like a space of your own to work on lessons and so forth. I can see I was wrong. We'll think no more of it. Come to the parlor and sit down."

I stopped, and she stopped with me. I leaned back, my hand on the wall behind me. "Why are you being so kind to me?"

She smiled. "I think Conconully needs you."

I'd certainly had that impression last night. The only thing I could think was that they'd been so desperate for a schoolteacher they'd take anyone, sight unseen. But that still didn't explain–

Belinda went on. "It's pleasant to have someone to share my home again." She faltered, slightly. "And I like you."

"You barely know me." I could have bitten my tongue. And precisely how long had Jean known me before she'd invited me to board at her home? Certainly not less than twenty-four hours, I thought. But then if Jean were here, I knew what she'd be telling me. And she'd be right. "But I am very grateful for your kindness. The study is lovely, and if you have no need for it yourself I would like to make use of it. Thank you for making me feel so welcome."

Belinda and I were discussing the terms of my lease, or at least I was trying to, when a knock sounded on the door. She went to answer it, and, gratefully, because I could recognize a losing argument when I saw one, I went to the sink to do the washing up. But only a moment later, Belinda was back. "I told you I'd do that," she said. "Besides, Doctor Amy is here, and she wants to take a look at you."

I did not move, as I did not want to give up what little ground I'd managed to gain. "Good morning, Doctor, but I really am much better this morning."

"Humor me," Amy said, and picked up a dish towel. "Dry your hands and come with me. You can't start your teaching position until I give you a clean bill of health."

My breath caught. Was this little dream to end so abruptly?

"Come on. It's only a formality. We don't want you fainting in front of your classroom or something."

"Go on," Belinda added from where she'd taken over the chore.

"There's no point," I said miserably. I would have to confess, and my world was going to fall apart. Again.

But Amy took me firmly by the arm, not at all like Belinda's bolstering touch, and led me out of the kitchen and up the stairs. "Which one is your room?"

I gestured. She all but dragged me into it and pointed at the bed, waited until I sat down on it, then pulled the chair out of the corner and sat facing me. I could not meet her earnest gaze, and stared down at my hands, knotted together on my lap.

"Look, Claudia, I know and you know you had something wrong with you when you came here. Something bad. Do you know what your illness was?"

"Is," I choked out. "Not was. I'm dying."

"Can you look at me?" Her voice was gentle.

I shook my head mutely.

I heard the breath go out of her. "Do you know what you were dying *of?*"

I swallowed. Why did she speak of it as if I was no longer ill? "A tumor in my womb, the specialist said. But he told me I waited too long, and it's spread. There's nothing to be done."

Silence for a long moment, then she asked briskly, "How do you feel now? Are you in pain? Do you feel weak or faint?"

I thought about it, taking stock. "No, not right now." I felt better than I had in months, which was very odd. Aside from my tongue, which had not quite recovered from Belinda's cooking, I felt very good indeed. I lifted my head. "No. No pain." I stared at her. "How can that be?"

Instead of responding to my question, she closed her eyes for a moment. When she opened them again, her entire demeanor had changed, to something reminiscent of the specialist in Seattle right before he'd told me I was dying. My breath caught in my throat. And then she asked me a question that made no sense whatsoever. "Are you happy?"

As if my happiness had anything whatsoever to do with the discussion or my health or my fitness for my new position.

I stared at her, speechless. At last, I said the only thing I could think of. "I-I don't understand."

"But it *is* important, isn't it? " She sounded so earnest, as if happiness was the goal of every human being. Perhaps, in an ideal world it ought to be, but given I'd lost everything, my position, my dreams, my home – *Jean*, a little voice whispered in my ear – and had come here to the back of beyond because I had no choice, only to find a place so mysteriously peculiar it frightened me. But it also fascinated me, and here I was, with a new job, and a new home, surrounded by people who seemed genuinely glad I was here, and feeling better than I had in months–

The young doctor broke into my mental confusion. "You can't truly be well unless you're happy."

"I-I suppose not."

But she was smiling at me again. "At any rate, I do hope you still want to take over our school. Half the town is up at the schoolhouse right now, cleaning things up and making repairs. Can you start tomorrow?"

That was sudden, but then I thought about what I'd seen of the town so far. "Will the school be habitable by then?"

She laughed out loud. "It will be as ready as you are."

Against my will, I could not help laughing with her. Just then, Belinda peered around the jamb of the open door, smiling. "Now that is a pleasant sound."

"I have given our new teacher a clean bill of health," Amy said, rising. "I'd say that's a good reason to be pleased."

It made no sense. None of it did. But I was not about to look a gift horse in the mouth, nor to do anything to jeopardize my new position.

Doctor Amy left soon thereafter, after telling me to rest for the remainder of the day, but while I knew I should not overtax myself, I had never felt less like resting in my life.

"I want to go see the school," I told Belinda, but she shook her head.

"Tomorrow will be soon enough."

I couldn't help protesting. "I can't simply walk in and start teaching without preparation. I need to see what books there are at the very least, and what records the last teacher left about the pupils and so forth."

But another knock sounded on the front door. "I must see who that is," Belinda said. "Do as the doctor says, Claudia. You'll need your energy tomorrow." She waited precisely long enough for me to nod reluctant assent, then left the room.

I heard Belinda and a voice I did not recognize, their conversation sounding like a business transaction. A few moments after that I heard an odd whirring sound I realized was the hum, muffled by the walls between us, of one of the sewing machines. It brought back memories of my mother sewing for us when I was a child. Comforting, somehow.

This reminded me. I had not yet unpacked my valise. I could at least do that before I disobeyed the little doctor, because I had no intention of leaving my curiosity unsatisfied.

It did not take long for me to empty my valise into the wardrobe and dresser. Looking around in satisfaction, I picked up my handbag. Once downstairs, I glanced over at Belinda's workroom door, but it was still closed, the whirring noise emanating from behind it unabated. Good, I thought, and headed for the front entry, only to be distracted by the open doorway to the room Belinda had designated as my office. I could not help but go inside, drawn by the desk under the window.

I had always wanted a desk like that, had envied Jean hers, and I'm afraid I spent more time than I should have exploring all the cubbyholes and shelves and trying the key that locked one of the drawers. Yes, it did lock. It wasn't as if I had anything to keep secret, but it made me feel like a child hiding her candy as I tucked the key into the outer pocket of my handbag.

A knock sounded on the front door. Another of Belinda's customers? The sewing machine kept whirring, so I pulled myself away to go answer it.

"Hello." Another stranger, everyone was a stranger here, but this one was a young boy, perhaps ten years old.

"Hi! I'm Brian!" He positively bounced on the balls of his feet, even with his arms full of a stack of books of all sizes and shapes, ranging from an atlas at the bottom to a bluebacked speller at the top, tucked under his chin.

I could not help but smile at him. "Hello, Brian."

"You're Miss Ogden, right? The new teacher?"

"Yes, I am." I reached for the stack of books, as it teetered and threatened to fall. "Would you like to come in?"

He shook his head, but he also refused to let go of his cargo, even as the top three or four volumes slid, dangerously close to escaping the stack altogether.

"You might wish to make a decision," I said, then the books made it for him, slipping and sliding and landing all over the worn gray boards of the front stoop.

"Oh! I'm sorry, Teacher!"

When the books, none the worse for wear, were gathered up again, the books safely on the little table just inside the door, I said, "It's all right. Are you sure you won't come in?"

I could see his curiosity, but he said emphatically, "Oh, no, ma'am."

"Will I see you in school tomorrow?"

His equilibrium was apparently restored by my question. "Yes, ma'am!"

I watched him bounce down the street, joined by several other boys, who apparently hadn't been quite brave enough to knock on the teacher's door. A distinct, "She's *nice!*" floated back on the morning breeze. I smiled as I went back inside to carry my new treasure to my new desk. Riches, indeed.

CHAPTER 8

The pile consisted mostly of textbooks. The speller, several McGuffey Readers of various levels, an arithmetic book, and a few others. An atlas and an almanac from a decade or so ago rounded out the stack. Adequate, if not ideal. Perhaps I could take a look in Dr. Duvall's unofficial library and see what else I could borrow for the purpose.

I sat down to examine them, one by one. None of the books was dated later than 1892, which would not do at all. I guessed up-to-date classroom materials were not a priority for whoever made the determination as to what Oscar Miller brought in those barrels. I decided, then and there, that I would discuss this with Mr. Pepper and see what could be done about it, but in the meantime I could make do.

The last book was a ledger, of a type I was quite familiar with, having used one almost identical to it to keep track of attendance and grades in the one-room schoolhouse I'd taught near my parents' home in Montana before coming to Seattle. It contained records, dating back for– that was odd. No years were listed. No dates at all, for that matter. Just half a dozen page spreads, filled out with names and checkmarks for attendance which corresponded to roughly a normal-length term on the left, and, on the opposing page, headings for reading, arithmetic, and so on, with grades opposite the corresponding name.

I turned each page slowly, studying the list of names, which did not change. Neither did the grades. Very odd. Peculiar, in fact. Why had someone copied the information from the same term over and over?

Until I reached the last page. The handwriting on it, listing the exact same information as the five spreads before it, jumped out at me as if it were printed in colored light. I knew that handwriting, or thought I did.

I raised my hand to my open mouth. The page curled up as if to hide itself, and hastily I spread my hand to flatten it again.

It could not possibly be Jean's handwriting. Jean was no teacher. It had been all she could do to maintain what she'd called her 'cover' during her stint researching her exposé on the Seattle schools. Even with my tutelage she'd almost discovered herself to Miss Taylor's predecessor at least twice. Moreover, she'd hated teaching. Hated everything about it, the drudgework as well as everything that made that part of the job worthwhile. Hated even the parts that gave me joy.

Handwriting was unique, but that did not mean it was reliably distinguishable, I told myself. I could and would ask who my predecessor had been, and I would be told, and it would not be Jean. *Could* not be Jean. I needed to put that ridiculous notion out of my mind. She had grown up here, and she knew Mr. Pepper and Mr. Miller, but she'd left here long ago.

I was glad someone had thought to have the boy Brian bring the books to me. I studied the ledger again. I would have a large class, some thirty-two children. Far more than I would have expected in a place like this. Then again, I had never lived in a place like this. I suspected no other place like this existed. The children ranged in age from five to seventeen. I'd be back in a one-room schoolhouse again. I could not help but smile.

* * *

I had still thought to make my way to the schoolhouse that afternoon, to look over my new domain, and help with bringing it back into order, but when noon came I decided I would anticipate Belinda and make something a bit more edible first. But when I went into the kitchen, I was surprised to discover Mrs. Missel there before me. On the table was a tureen, from which wafted delicious odors, and she was slicing a loaf of bread. Its shape and size looked familiar from the one I'd eaten from at breakfast.

"Hello."

"Good afternoon." Her eyes glinted as she smiled up at me. "You look rather relieved."

And what was I to say to that? Surely she knew, but– "Do you normally cook for Belinda?"

"She's working on Amy's wedding dress, and she has a tendency to forget to eat when she gets wrapped up in something. But you both need your sustenance."

I can cook, I wanted to tell her, but did not. It seemed ungrateful, and the soup smelled so good. "Thank you," I said instead.

"Sit down. I'll go let Belinda know I've brought the meal." Mrs. Missel left, and I did as I was told. A moment later the whirring which had been the everpresent background to my morning stopped, and Mrs. Missel spoke, then Belinda. I could not tell what they were saying from this distance, but it began to sound more like an argument than anything else. At last they both came in.

"You should have started without me," Belinda said. To me, or to Mrs. Missel? She sounded a bit peeved. "I was right in the middle of those tucks."

"And if I'd left you there, you'd still be in the middle of them by suppertime."

"Well, it's water over the dam now." Belinda sat down. Mrs. Missel made to pick up the ladle, but Belinda waved her off. "We can serve ourselves." She sighed, the sound more exasperated than anything else. "But I do thank you, Audrey. Go feed your husband. I'm sure he's waiting for you."

Mrs. Missel left, with a sniff and an "I'm sure you're quite welcome."

"She means well," Belinda said with another sigh, this one mitigated a bit by her look of anticipation as she dished up what turned out to be a rich, thick chicken soup filled with vegetables.

I handed round the bread, and we dug in.

"Does she often cook for you?" I asked after I'd satisfied my first hunger. I certainly hoped so.

"A few times a week." Belinda grimaced. "Today I think she wanted to make sure you don't starve."

"I would be more than happy to cook, too," I told her.

"We'll take turns."

I let that one go, but I determined then and there that my turn would come round far more often than hers would.

It was a pleasant lunch, and not just because of the food. Belinda told me about her wagon trip west back in the days before the railroads came to Washington, and the story of how she'd wound up in Conconully.

"I'd heard such lovely things about this town, and every one of them turned out to be correct," she said. "The people, the climate, and the church. Of course," she added with a self-deprecating smile, "the fact that the town was hurting for a good seamstress did not discourage me one bit. I settled here not long after the mines opened and the first settlers came, and I've been happy here ever since."

Happy. Was it a coincidence that Amy had asked me if I was happy? But before I could say anything about it, Belinda declared, "But I have been monopolizing the conversation. Tell me about yourself, and what brought you to Conconully."

What could I say? "I came here looking for work."

She beamed at me. "And you've found it."

Yes, I had. I had never had a position fall so magically into my lap before. One that was so well-suited for me, and I for it. "My friend Jean Clancy told me you were looking for a teacher here. She used to live in Conconully. Did you know her?"

Did a shadow pass over Miss Houseman's face, or did I imagine it? "I remember the family," she said at last. "Six children, if I recall correctly. They did not stay. The children grew up and moved away, and once they were gone, the parents left, too. Back before the flood."

Flood? This was the second time someone had mentioned it. "I have a photograph," I told her, and rose to go fetch it.

"Do you?" But she seemed profoundly uninterested in seeing it, and I sat back down.

"Do you enjoy teaching?" she asked me, and I relaxed for the moment. It was a comfortable subject, and a question I could answer in the affirmative without a qualm.

"Yes, I do. I taught third grade at a grammar school in Seattle."

"Seattle has become a large city, has it not?"

"Yes, ever since the Klondike Gold Rush it has been growing by leaps and bounds. The school district has built three new schools in the last five years, trying to keep up with all of the new children. And hiring the teachers to fill them. This is-" I steadied my voice with an effort "-was to be my second year teaching there."

"Where did you live before that?"

"In Montana." I paused to consider Malta in comparison. "In a small town almost as remote as Conconully."

She smiled. "Not too many places can lay claim to being more remote than Conconully."

I smiled back ruefully. "True."

"Were you happy in your small town?" It seemed the first question in which she had a sincere interest, not simply asking to be polite.

That word again. People here seemed obsessed with it. "I miss it. But there was no room for me there. And I wanted to see the world."

"And have you?"

"Seen the world? Not really." I remembered when I'd traveled to Havre in my father's wagon, to stay with my aunt and uncle while I attended teacher's college. Returning to Malta to teach, feeling like I'd never left, and would never leave again. Defying my parents by purchasing a one-way rail ticket to Seattle. How frightened I'd been, and how brave I'd felt. How, almost in spite of myself, I'd missed the camaraderie of a small town, and of family, and friends, and people who'd known me since I was a small child, but how I couldn't admit defeat and return. How I'd managed to find my niche in the school district, at least, but how lonely I'd been until I'd met Jean Clancy. How thrilled I had been when she'd befriended me and how I'd hoped for more.

How desolate I'd been to have my hopes dashed.

"Do you still wish to travel?"

It was only a polite question again, I supposed, but I gave it more thought than the query warranted. And, oddly enough, the conclusion I came to was not the one I would have thought. "No." What I wanted was to belong somewhere again, I realized in surprise. "Travel is too full of strangers."

Miss Houseman nodded at me as if my odd statement made perfect sense to her. I nodded back. What else could I do?

"Do you wish to go back to Montana?"

Again, a question I should have answered lightly, but– "No," I said again. "Montana is my past."

She nodded at me again, in what looked like some satisfaction. "You are looking for a future."

"Yes."

The next morning, bright and early, I closed the front door of Belinda's house behind me and climbed the small hill to my new place of employment. The sun was barely up behind me, the snow-capped peaks to the west pink with dawn. On the other side of those mountains lay Seattle, huddling under the gray, scudding rain clouds of November. But here the sky was clear and blue, the breeze promising warmth as the day wore on, even as my breath puffed out in little bursts of steam into the dry, crisp air.

The schoolhouse, like every other building I passed on my way, showed its age but was not as tumbledown as I had expected from my first sight of town two days ago. It was freshly coated with whitewash, and its windows were whole and shining. I could see where several boards on the steps had been repaired and the doorknob replaced with gleaming brass hardware. Whoever had done the work had made a skillful and fast job of it. I wondered if- no, I would make it a point to find out who had made the repairs, and I would find some tangible way to thank him. But for now, I had my own work to do.

I had thought to arrive before all of my students, but young Brian had turned up before me and was in the process of laying a fire in the freshly-blacked stove when I came in. I set the brand-new satchel Belinda had given me yesterday evening much to my surprise onto the freshly-wiped desk at the front of the room, and looked around in pleasure.

The chalkboard behind my desk had been freshly repainted and given a new rail, with a number of new pieces of chalk resting on it. A line of windows ran down the sides of the room, bright in the morning light. Rows of desks, each one linked to the one behind it, looked to be adequate in number for the students I expected. At the back of the room, a bucket stood on a bench with a dipper hanging from a hook on the wall next to it. Of course.

The school where I taught in Seattle had boasted running water and electricity, but I should not have expected it here. I could see the outhouse through the window as well.

"I'll fill that, Teacher," Brian told me when I made to take the bucket— where? Back to Belinda's house, where there was a pump in the kitchen?

"Thank you." He was inordinately helpful for a boy his age. "Is this your job?" I asked him.

His smile dimmed for a moment. He nodded, and scooted out the door with the bucket.

I shook my head and went back to the teacher's desk to prepare for my day.

By the time Brian returned, children filled the schoolyard. The school even had an old-fashioned bell to ring to call them in for class. I truly did feel as if I had been transported back to Malta and my own schooldays. I picked it up and rang it, more than satisfied when the children formed two neat lines, girls and boys, and filed past my approving gaze to their desks.

The first duty of any teacher is to get to know her pupils, to learn their names and to find out where they are along the road to knowledge. I spent a pleasurable morning in that pursuit, assisting the small ones as they read from their primers and watching them do simple sums, and having the older ones recite history, geography, and perform more complicated mathematics. By the end of the morning I was quite favorably impressed with a class of scholars who had not backslid even in what I knew must be difficult circumstances.

I dismissed them to their midday meal, and stood in the doorway watching them career down the hill like a flock of birds. When I went to fetch my shawl, however, I found young Brian still there, still in his seat.

"You need to go home and eat," I told him.

"May I stay here?"

"Why? Aren't you hungry?" Now that I took the time to observe him, I began to wonder if he had a home to return to. I should have noticed the signs before. It was not as if I was unfamiliar with them. A child from poor circumstances stands out like a weed in the garden if one knows what to look for. The clothing, yes. His were too small and too worn, his shoes in particular bulging in places where they should not be. His face, thinner than it should be, and his hair untrimmed. His obvious good cheer, both yesterday and today, had been so bright it had distracted me from the obvious.

"Would you like to come and have lunch with me?" I asked.

His eyes lit for a moment, then dimmed. "No, thank you."

"Why not? You would be my guest." I knew this sort of pride, too. I had felt it as a child, inculcated by my parents, who had done their best by us and wanted no charity. "You could help me a great deal. As a stranger in town, there is so much I need to know." And was that not the truth, not that I expected young Brian to have the answers to the questions I needed most.

To my surprise, my appeal to his expertise did not provoke the response I expected.

His eyes went wide. He shook his head, and darted past me out the door.

I called after him, but by the time I collected my shawl and headed out, he was gone.

CHAPTER 9

"Do you know a young man named Brian?" I asked. It wasn't what I'd expected to say. I'd arrived home from school for lunch expecting to make my own meal, only to find Belinda, unlike yesterday, in the kitchen before me. She wasn't cooking, fortunately, but only setting out the makings for sandwiches. Roast beef, pickles, and lettuce that looked as if it had arrived from the garden this morning.

But the boy Brian was more important.

Belinda turned, plates in her hands. "No, I don't. How was your first morning in the classroom?"

Well, and so. She wanted to talk about one thing, and I another. The situation reminded me of many similar conversations I'd had with Jean, and I almost laughed at Belinda's transparency. "It was fine. The reason I ask is he seems to be in need of proper care. Clothing and food and so forth. Is there any way to find out where he lives? I would like to speak to his parents."

She set the plate down on the table. "I'm sorry, I need to get back to work. I'll take my sandwich with me."

And with that, she was gone, plate in hand, through the door to her workroom. I got up to follow her, to apologize, but as I reached the workroom door and peered in, I saw her, sandwich neglected, a fierce scowl on her face, her foot pumping the treadle so fast it looked like a blur.

I backed away to the kitchen and sat down to my own sandwich. I would apologize to her this evening, although what I had done to upset her I could not imagine. But my own time was in short supply. I barely made it back to the schoolhouse in time to ring the bell and start classes that afternoon.

The boy Brian was not there. And when I asked my other students about him, including two of the boys I'd seen whispering with him that morning, they only gave me blank stares. It wasn't that they were lying to me. It was as if I was asking them about a ghost.

I would not give up on this, but for now, with thirty-one children in my classroom, I could not pursue the subject until later. I filed my concern away and concentrated on the children in front of me.

The mystery of the boy Brian aside, my first day in Conconully's one-room schoolhouse was most satisfying. There is nothing more wonderful, in my opinion, than making progress with students who truly want to learn. Even the small disciplines I'd had to hand out were only a slight distraction.

I had almost forgotten about Brian by the time the day was over. Almost, but not quite. I stood in the doorway of the school building, watching the children scatter as they ran down the hill toward their homes, enjoying that good feeling of having made a difference. And the view.

The prospect from the school presented a different angle from the hill where I'd first viewed the town. And more than that. The settlement did not look quite so rundown now as I had thought it when I first arrived. Perhaps I had simply been too critical. The bright spring afternoon sun shone down on buildings and streets that perhaps had fallen on hard times, but were certainly not as deserted-looking as I had thought they were. Perhaps the town had simply needed people to look as if it were alive, and not long dead.

I smiled at my fancy, but as I remembered my concern for the missing young boy, it faded. I had a legitimate reason to explore. To see where I would be staying until I could find a way out. I needed to find Brian, and see to his welfare.

Locks did not seem to be something people used here, or, rather, I had not seen any keys, either for the house I was staying in or for the schoolhouse itself. I supposed in a hamlet this tiny and remote, with no railroad running through bringing ruffians and roustabouts as we'd had in Malta, and certainly without the crowds of the big city I encountered regularly in Seattle, there was no need. I closed the schoolhouse door firmly behind me, and headed down the hill, as curious as I had been the evening I arrived here.

Even the path leading down from the schoolhouse into town seemed in better shape than it had been. But then that could have been part of the result of the work done on the building yesterday. It had been amazing, what the townspeople had accomplished in only a day.

I had forgotten what it was like to let myself be completely subsumed into the vocation I loved. I never been able to accomplish that in Seattle for more than a moment or two at a time. There were too many rules. Too much bureaucracy. Too much being watched over. Here, even on my first day, I'd been entrusted with thirty-two young lives, with no oversight whatsoever.

How did they know I was trustworthy?

I stopped halfway down the hill, my hand over my mouth, then shook my head. *I* knew I was trustworthy. The children would give a good report of me to their parents. And if the parents had questions, I knew I could answer them honestly to their satisfaction.

Which brought me back to my concern for Brian, and my urge to explore the town. Which goals were not mutually exclusive.

"Hello, Teacher!" I whirled at the familiar voice.

"Brian!"

He grinned at me, and, before I could stop him, he relieved me of my satchel of books and papers.

"Where were you this afternoon?"

His grin faded. "I had to work."

This was not acceptable. The state of Washington had recently enacted laws against child labor, and added a requirement for children to attend school until the age of sixteen. One step at a time, I thought. I would talk to his parents, speak with his putative employer, and resolve this problem. And if they did not cooperate, I would report them— I faltered. To whom? Surely the sheriff would back me up.

"Could you take me to your parents, Brian?"

He stared at the ground, and scraped one badly-shod foot against it.

I tried again. "I don't wish to cause you trouble, but I would like to meet them."

He mumbled something unintelligible. I was beginning to have suspicions I did not care for at all.

"Look at me, child. You've done nothing wrong. But I need to speak to your parents." I put a hand under his chin, and, yes, I'd seen that particular sheen in a child's eyes before. I knelt down in front of him. "Brian, where are they?"

"Don't know." His words now, compared to his cheery greeting, were almost inaudible.

Which could mean any of a number of things. He could be fibbing because he was afraid of being punished if I spoke to them. He could simply not know where they were right this moment, or this day, or this month, or this year. Or they could be gone altogether. Or dead. I softened my voice. "I was about to go back to my house and get something to eat. Would you like to come with me?"

"Shouldn't."

Whoever had told him so would need to be set straight as well. "Of course you should. I would like to discuss your employment."

He stared at me, but when I led the way back to Belinda's house, which I was beginning to think of as mine as well, he followed without argument.

He hesitated again at the door, but I gestured him inside, and once in, he gazed around in pleasure, much as I had when I'd first entered.

"Oh, Teacher, this is nice!"

I smiled at him. "You can set the satchel on the table." I headed toward the kitchen. "Come along."

It was not yet suppertime, but I was quite sure the boy could eat. I was feeling a bit peckish myself.

Brian hovered in the doorway, as if still unsure of his welcome. I gestured him in. "Make yourself at home." When he still hesitated, I added, "You are welcome here." If Belinda did not agree with me, then I would cross that bridge when I arrived there. But apparently Brian's experience was otherwise, or he would not have been so reluctant.

I opened a cupboard, not sure of what I would find there. Dishes, sturdy white china with a peculiar but pretty swirling pattern around the edges. I had not noticed the pattern last night or today. Odd. But then I had not been paying attention. I closed the cupboard again and opened another. Thick sturdy glasses, which I did recognize, and mugs to match the dishes.

"What do you like to eat?"

He had crept in while I was searching, and watched me as if I were a mirage. I smiled at him, and gestured at the table. He seated himself, even if on the very edge of the chair, as if to be ready to jump up and run away at any moment. I opened a third cupboard, and, at last, found foodstuffs. I found the rest of the loaf of that good, crusty bread, and a pot of jam. I pulled open a drawer and found a knife. "I'm going to have a bite. Would you like some?"

Brian nodded so vigorously his cap fell off of his head. When I gave him the food, he engulfed it like a starving boy. I wondered exactly how literal that hyperbolic phrase actually was, but I dared not risk asking him, for fear of scaring him off.

I served myself, and gave him a second helping, but bread and jam were not a solid meal. I glanced around the room, only then noticing the wooden chestlike piece in the corner. An icebox.

I set my bread back down and rose. "Would you light the stove for me, Brian?" But as I was about to open the icebox, the back door opened.

"Well," said Mrs. Missel. "I see you couldn't wait for supper." She held a tray loaded with several covered dishes.

I straightened. "I thought I'd invite Brian in for a bite to eat." I didn't want to embarrass him by saying he looked hungry or I thought he didn't have a home or anything else. His situation should have been obvious to anyone who looked at the boy, at any rate.

But Mrs. Missel gave me a blank look. "Oh, and will he be along soon? I'll set another plate."

I stared at her in turn, and, helplessly, over at the boy, who was in plain sight. I gestured, but my hand stopped in mid-air, as if of its own accord. Brian was shaking his head at me, a panicked expression on his face. And, before I could stop him, he slid out of his seat, bread and jam still grasped in his hand, and darted out the back door. "I-I suppose not," I said weakly. "I will be right back."

Leaving Mrs. Missel behind, her "hmph, such manners," floating in the air, I scanned the garden behind the house anxiously, looking not to simply find Brian, but catch him, bring him back to the cottage, and feed him a lecture on behavior along with Mrs. Missel's cooking.

Or perhaps not. He seemed to have vanished utterly. Not a footstep, not a snicker or giggle or even an indrawn breath. Not a rustle among the tall grass. Not anything.

Behind me, the kitchen door opened again. "Supper's ready," Mrs. Missel told me, her voice conveying her disapproval in no undertain terms. "Please fetch Belinda. You'll want to eat it before it grows cold."

Reluctantly, I cannot express how reluctantly, I followed her back inside. Something kept me from mentioning the boy Brian again. Mrs. Missel's forbidding expression, most likely. It reminded me of Father's when I had told him I wished to go to Seattle.

I reacted to Mrs. Missel precisely the way I'd reacted to Father two years ago. I dropped the subject, but not my thoughts on it, or my determination. If Belinda, and now Mrs. Missel, would not discuss the obvious needs of that poor boy, then I would find someone who would.

CHAPTER 10

So I went to fetch Belinda, who was, thank goodness, more amenable to coming to supper than she had been for lunch. Mrs. Missel had delivered chicken and dumplings, the latter so light and airy I wondered if they would slip free of their gravy bonds and take flight.

The food was delicious, but somehow insubstantial. I do not mean the dumplings were not light and airy as the best dumplings are, or the chicken was not tender and juicy as it should have been. But even the vegetables tasted as if I was eating cotton candy, not sweet, but almost disappearing in my mouth before I could chew and swallow them.

Belinda did not appear to notice anything out of the ordinary, but she didn't have much to say, either, seemingly preoccupied with something, perhaps a complication with the wedding dress. I finished my share of the meal in spite of myself, down to my slice of strawberry cake, then rose.

"I need to go out for a bit," I told her. "I'll do the washing up when I get back."

She merely shrugged, then rose herself and headed back to her workroom. Well, I thought, no one can be cheerful all the time, and went out.

I would find the sheriff. He would know what to do to find the boy and bring him in so he could be cared for. It was what would be done in Seattle, and what I should have done here as soon as I understood the situation.

I strode down the little side street toward the center of town, keeping a sharp eye out for places where a young boy might hide from his elders. If I could find him on my own, persuade him to come back, to let me help him, it would be simpler for all concerned. I suspected, however, that he'd run off to the woods.

The forest stood thickly around Conconully, not precisely encroaching upon it, but surrounding, and, I thought with a shiver on that warm spring evening, enclosing it. Hiding it from anyone who might accidentally wander nearby. Which was a fancy I did not need to consider.

My arrival had not been an accident, although it certainly had been unexpected by the local denizens. I wondered, suddenly, how important that distinction was here.

I had no idea where the sheriff might be at this hour of the evening. I was hesitant for some reason to ask the people I passed. I simply nodded and smiled at them as they did to me. One of my young students tugged on her mother's hand and pointed at me excitedly. Her mother smiled in embarrassment as she tugged the impolite little finger down and admonished her child, but before I could say anything, she bustled away.

Everyone's clothing and hair were as old-fashioned as Belinda's, and I supposed I could ascribe that to the remoteness of the place. But it still seemed odd to me. Surely at least one of those barrels had an issue or two of a lady's magazine, or even some newspapers.

It was then I spotted the sheriff, sitting on a swing hanging from the porch in front of a neat little white house, in good repair. Why had I not seen it when I first– Never mind.

He was not alone. Amy sat beside him. Their conversation, and the easy motion of the swing, stopped as I arrived at the foot of the two steps leading to the porch, directly in front of them.

"Good evening, Miss Ogden," said the sheriff. "Nice night for a stroll."

"I am not strolling," I told him, politely but firmly. "I am looking for someone. A young boy, one of my students."

"Did your first day go well, then?" Amy asked. She couldn't be trying to change the subject, could she?

"Very well indeed," I replied. What else could I say? "But about the boy Brian–"

This time she interrupted me outright. "I'm glad to hear it, but I'm not surprised."

"You barely know me–"

This time the sheriff interrupted me. Honestly, these two were being about as rude as rude could be. "Brian? That name sounds familiar– ow!" I stared at the two of them. She'd kicked him, of that I was quite sure. He glared over at her. "Look. You can't ignore the elephant in the room. Besides, you don't know– all right." This as she glared right back at him. They both rose, the sheriff steadying the swing for his fiancée. They headed for the door.

Apparently they were going to be rude enough to simply turn away and go inside. But as he reached for the doorknob, Amy glanced back at me and said, "Come on. This is something we really shouldn't talk about out here."

"Besides, there's cake inside," he added.

"Of course, Amy said, laughing, as the sheriff held the door for me.

"Hey, cake's important," he protested, and led the way down a short hall past a pretty little parlor on the right, to a door on the left leading to a kitchen that looked very much like the one in Belinda's house.

About half of what looked like the strawberry cake I'd eaten a slice of earlier sat on the table in the middle of the room. The sheriff went to a cupboard in the corner and fetched plates and cups, while Amy moved the kettle to the stove, which was still putting out some heat.

"Need more wood?" he asked.

"Yes, please."

He set the dishes on the table, took up the empty wood basket from its place beside the stove, and left.

I shook my head at Amy's offer of cake. "Mrs. Missel brought slices with supper. It was delicious, but two slices in one day would be a bit much."

She nodded agreement, but went ahead and took some for herself, and cut a rather large slab, presumably for the sheriff.

This might, I thought, be a good time to bring up something else, while we waited for his return. I hadn't quite had the gumption to bring it up with Belinda herself, but–"Does Miss Houseman pay Mrs. Missel to do her cooking? Much as I've enjoyed it, and I certainly do not wish to hurt Mrs. Missel's feelings or deprive her of a source of income, I rather like cooking for myself and would not mind in the least doing it for the two of us. Do you think it too forward of me to bring the subject up with either of them?" I hesitated, but it was nothing more than the facts. "Mrs. Missel didn't even seem to like it when I buttered a slice of bread for myself and Brian after school this afternoon. I don't know if it would hurt her feelings if I said anything."

Amy, who'd just taken a bite of her cake without waiting for her fiancé's return, gave me a startled look and set her fork down, but she chewed and swallowed before answering. Actually, she sat there for a moment after swallowing, as if wondering what to say.

The sheriff chose that moment to return, opening the stove and adding wood from the basket onto the coals. "Kettle's boiling, and I thought the fire was out, but I guess not. Want me to pour?"

"Sure," Amy told him We both watched him as he carefully transferred the steaming water from kettle to teapot, then brought the pot over to the table.

"Looks like you beat me to it." He took a bite from the slab of cake at his place, then set his fork down and looked at Amy, then at me. "Okay. Out with it."

"She doesn't want Audrey to cook for her," Amy said, sounding rather more incredulous than was needful.

"She *what?*" the sheriff – Dan, he'd asked me to call him, I reminded myself – all but spluttered.

"She," I said into the vacuum that followed, "has enjoyed Audrey's cooking," I did not add, despite its insubstantiality which I could not explain, "but actually likes to cook for herself."

Dan laughed. "Unlike someone we know whose name we won't mention?"

I hadn't meant it as an insult– "I'm sorry, I didn't mean to imply–"

But Amy was laughing, too, if a bit shamefacedly. "I don't think Audrey will be offended." She sobered, then took a deep breath. "I don't think the food was what offended her this afternoon."

I sat there puzzled for a moment, then light dawned. "Brian. She was offended I would feed that child. What on earth could he have done to *her* for her to treat him that way?"

Amy looked helplessly at Dan. "It's really too soon to be getting into this."

"I don't think we have a choice." He turned to look straight at me, his cake forgotten in front of him. "Miss Ogden, Audrey wasn't offended. She was upset. And the reason she was upset was because young Brian Whittaker died in the flood."

It was a very good thing I was sitting down at that moment. I am fairly certain I would have landed on the floor. As it was, the world went a bit gray, and, for a moment, all I could see was the ruin of the building around me, decrepit as though no one had lived there for years. The roof open to the sky where it had collapsed, the stove encrusted in rust, a bird's nest poking out of the broken stove pipe, and the chair I was seated in suddenly wobbling beneath me, as if no longer capable of holding my weight. I reached desperately for the table, but it was gone. And I was utterly alone.

Then everything snapped back, with a sudden effort that made my heart skip one beat, then a second, before it suddenly started pounding erratically. I gasped, unable to catch my breath. Another snap, back to ruin. I squeezed my eyes closed.

Then Amy's voice. "Quick, go get Max. Something's really wrong."

A door slam. Arms catching me. I knew they were Amy's, but I barely felt them. Then I blacked out

When I woke, the morning light was streaming through my bedroom window. Morning? I was in the bed in the house I was beginning to think of as ours, not just Belinda's, but the last thing I remembered was being seated at the sheriff's kitchen table, in his house? office? and –

"How are you feeling?" At least I recognized the young doctor's voice. "You gave us quite a scare last night."

"I am sorry, " I said automatically. "I don't remember–" but suddenly I did. "Brian cannot be dead. I've seen him. I've spoken with him. He attended school yesterday and came in to have a snack with me, then Mrs. Missel arrived and he ran off. He's very much alive, I promise you."

I started to get up, but Amy rose from her chair and gently – surprising me with how weak I truly was – pushed me back down.

"I need to find him," I told her, almost desperately. To prove it, myself, something.

"You're not in any shape to go looking for anyone, I promise you," she said firmly.

"He'll be at the schoolhouse. And what about the other children?"

But she was shaking her head. "You can't teach in the shape you're in right now."

She was right, I supposed. But I did not have to like it. Had the little doctor been wrong about my cancer? It had seemed far too good to be true when she'd proclaimed me fit to teach, but I had latched onto her positive diagnosis like a woman drowning who had been dragged from the water. I had felt better. I *had*. And even now I did not feel as I had before. I felt faint, and helpless, more as I had when I'd caught pneumonia as a child. Not in constant pain. Not in pain at all. Just so tired...

I fell back asleep far too easily, and could do nothing but allow it.

I dreamed, too, of Jean coming to me here, then wrapping her arms around me, only letting go to look up at me and smile and say, well, kiddo, it's about time you figured things out. I know I was crying, even in my dream, crying because I knew it was only a dream and, inexplicably, I so wished it could be real, that I could be back in Seattle with her, even though I knew I was better off, happier, here.

I woke again to a handkerchief blotting away my tears. I turned away from those gentle hands, knowing their owner felt pity for me, and I did not want pity.

"Here now," said a voice. Belinda. Amy would have been bad enough, but for Belinda to witness this– "Go away, please," I managed. My voice cracked, and I closed my mouth on the sound as if to hide it.

"Come along now," she said. I wanted to sink through the bedclothes into invisibility, like the boy Brian, I thought suddenly, and never come up again.

Belinda, who had been part of that dream, too, and now I wasn't even sure if the woman in my dream had been Jean or her. "Please. Go away."

"I promised Doc Amy I would stay. You wouldn't have me break a promise, would you?" She pulled gently at my shoulder and I rolled back over, fairly against my will. "Open your eyes now. You need to eat. I brought you a good soup."

I drew in my breath and opened my eyes. Belinda was smiling at me, the concern in her eyes belying her cheerful expression. But even as I watched the worry eased.

She proffered a spoonful of, if I must be honest, something rather strong-smelling.. It was either eat the soup or have it spill down my front, but I knew what was coming, and it was all I could do not to cringe.

When I opened my mouth the taste fell on my tongue like a battering ram. To this day, I am still not sure what it was supposed to be – the only flavor I could discern was enough spice, mostly pepper, of course, to sear the skin off of my tongue and make me cry in earnest.

I flailed my arms, gasping, perspiration breaking out on my forehead, and I could have sworn, my hair standing on end to try to escape.

Belinda handed me a glass of milk. I gulped it, and breathed again. She gave me a slice of bread, looking disappointed, the offered me the spoon again.

I shook my head vehemently, all thoughts of politeness gone in the pursuit of survival. "No, thank you," I finally managed.

She sighed. "Ah, well. But it did wake you up completely. How do you feel now?"

I took mental inventory. To my surprise, I did feel better. Stronger. Certainly well enough to get out of bed.

"Well? How did your experiment go, Miss Houseman?" The speaker was Mr. Pepper, who I had not seen since the day I'd arrived here, and he stood in the doorway, his short, stout form neatly clad in an elegantly pinstriped suit. He held his hat in his hands, and nodded at me. "Miss Ogden?"

I did not shriek and dive back under the covers, even though I wanted to. I merely pulled them up to my chin instead. "I am not fit for company at the moment, sir." I added to Belinda, "any company."

"Oh, come now, I'm not company, am I? Run along, Max, and wait in the parlor. I will send her to you shortly."

Max grinned, but left, whether to obey orders or not I did not know. Or care, at the moment.

"Here." Belinda tugged at the covers. "Let me help you."

I was tempted to, but not for the reasons she thought. Her vile concoction had indeed woken me up.

I swallowed, feeling abruptly as if I were betraying a confidence, although I could not have said why. Jean had been my friend; indeed, I would not be here if it were not for her. I would not be living in this odd but pleasant little town, or be gainfully employed, or have made the acquaintance of several agreeable individuals, including the kind woman who had taken me in, and was tending to me while neglecting her own business in the process.

I suppose that is why I suddenly felt so guilty. Taking me in as a boarder did not mean she was my keeper. Neither did the fact that I was beginning to think of her as a friend.

"I can manage on my own, thank you," then, realizing how stiff I sounded, tried to apologize. "I can, truly. Please tell Mr. Pepper I will be out to see him in a moment, then—" and how did I tell her to go on without sounding ungrateful? "I know you have work you need to be doing. I do not wish to be in your way."

I would not interpret the glance she gave me as hurt feelings. I would not. But all she said was, "All right," and let me to my own devices, to find my clothing and dress myself, to try to do something with the tangled mass of my hair.

I realized some moments later when I caught myself smoothing my skirt for the third time that I was dawdling. In dread? Of what? And strode purposefully to the parlor.

Belinda was not there, thank goodness, and I could hear the thrum of her sewing machine from behind the closed door to her workshop.

Yes, it was dread I was feeling, although I could not possibly picture anyone with a less threatening aspect than Max Pepper.

CHAPTER 11

He rose to greet me, from one of the pair of green-upholstered wing chairs near the now-lit parlor stove. He stepped forward, took my hand, and drew me toward the other one. "Sit. We should talk."

Something in that voice, kind-sounding though it was, brooked no refusal. I settled myself in the chair and he smiled at me. "Now at least you don't look as if you're going to run off any second." He paused. "Although your eyes still look as if you want to."

He reseated himself, leaning forward and regarding me earnestly. I suppose I could have pulled my own gaze away from him, but I suspected the act would be painful. Painful? Why? Tentatively, cautiously, I tried it, glancing down at my lap then back to him. Perhaps painful had not been the right word, but it had been more– unpleasant, than such a simple act should have been.

His lips curved again and he reached over to pat my hand. "You *are* welcome here. It's just you're an anomaly. Some here don't know what to do with such things."

An odd thing to call me, but I had the sudden feeling I had been an anomaly all my life. Until now. I shook it off. "What about the boy

Brian? He's *not* dead. I spoke to him only yesterday. Unless something has happened to him since then–"

"No, no," he hesitated, his expression gone completely serious. "You're the first person I know of who has seen him since the flood. I think that makes you someone we've never seen here before. A change." His face cleared. "Another change. A welcome one this time."

"You're making no sense." Being welcome in this place was *not* something I wished to aspire to at the moment.

"I am sorry." But he didn't look in the least penitent. "We've gotten so used to– Daniel was right," he interrupted himself. "That doesn't make it any easier."

Silence fell. After a moment I said, "Go on." I wasn't sure I wanted him to, but I was also certain I needed to know.

"What year is it, Miss Ogden?" The question was an utter non sequitur, and it caught me off guard.

"1910, of course," I told him impatiently.

He opened his mouth, then closed it again without speaking. After a moment, he said, his voice sounding rather choked, "1910." And shook his head. "I'm not sure if that explains anything or just makes it more confusing."

What I said next came out more tartly than I meant it to, which is saying a fair amount. "You cannot possibly be more confused than I am right now."

He laughed. "No, I suppose not. Will you listen to a story? A sort of fable, actually."

Somehow I did not think I had a choice. "All right."

The relief on his face was all out of proportion to the matter of fact tone of his voice. "All right then, Miss Ogden. Once upon a time, in a remote but bustling gold-mining camp in the mountains of Washington Territory, there lived two men. One was happily married, a teamster who brought goods to the camp from the river port fifteen miles away, who never aspired to riches or fame, but loved his wife and was happy in his life, even though they'd never had the children they'd longed for.

"The other man, not to put too fine a point on it, was a confidence man who longed for riches and fame, but did not wish to put in the honest labor to earn them. He arrived in the camp, which had become a town with the discovery of gold and the influx of miners. And those who earned their living mining those miners.

"You see," and here Mr. Pepper's gaze darted away from me for the first time since he'd begun his fable, "the confidence man had a plan, and he needed the teamster's help – or rather that of his wagon and mules – to carry it out.

"He staked a claim, out away from the existing mines, in the unlikeliest of places, and made a great show of prospecting and digging, and another when he hitched a ride to the land office in Omak to register that claim. Except he never did register it. Instead, he used the time with the teamster to tell him of the doctors in Seattle who might be able to help his wife carry a child, if only the teamster had the riches to pay for her treatment.

"The teamster would do anything for his beloved wife, and so, reluctantly, he agreed to help the confidence man. He would bring the confidence man's barrels, filled with iron pyrites, worthless stones which look like gold to the untrained eye, to his mine, and help salt the mine with them. Then the confidence man would sell the claim for many times what it was worth and they would split the profit.

"But when the two men, leaving the teamster's wagon in the meadow, the mules cropping the sweet May grass, went into the mine, which was really a natural cave, saving the confidence man the effort of digging, they found themselves drawn farther and farther into the deep dark until the only light came from their lanterns.

"Suddenly the teamster stopped, because a rock blocked his way. A large, very oddly-shaped rock. 'It's a pig,' he said, and without thought, dropped the heavy load of pyrites he was carrying, and hefted the rock in his arms. 'I will take this back for my wife.'"

"Why," I had to ask.

The little man shook his head. "I don't know. I don't know if she merely had an affection for pigs, or if– well, but I am ahead of my tale.

"The confidence man couldn't see the sense in it, but he couldn't see the harm in it, either. Where they stood was as good a place as any to stage their 'discovery,' so while the teamster carried the pig-shaped rock back to his wagon, he scattered the pyrites in an artistic manner, then left the cave himself, satisfied with his day's work.

"But when he walked out of the cave, the sun was high in the sky. It wasn't possible, as they'd entered the cave after nightfall, and only stayed there for an hour or so, but the evidence was undeniable. They hurried back to town, the confidence man leaving the teamster behind with his wagon and mules and pig, and ran down the valley, the better to display his excitement at his incredible 'find.'

"But when he arrived back in town, he could find no one with whom to share his simulated discovery. It was as if the town had been deserted overnight, until he heard singing coming from the whitewashed church. He was about to burst in on the service, for he had no shame in such matters, when he heard another sound. A loud roar. And he turned to find a solid wall of water rushing down the valley, headed straight for the town.

"The confidence man, I am sorry to say, did not stay on course for the church, but ran for the hotel and the possessions he had left there. But he did not reach it in time, either. He was washed away in that flood, on the 27th of May, 1893.

"It wasn't until later that he realized–"

I interrupted again. "He didn't die in the flood?"

"Death," said the little man, "is not as black and white as we think it is." He went on before I could ask him what on earth he meant by *that*.

"Here in Conconully, the entire town was washed away. Only two people I know of survived. The teamster," and here his gaze became encouraging, rather as if he were the teacher and I the child he was coaxing to decipher meaning from the words I was hearing, "and a small boy named Brian, who, it now seems, must have been hiding in the schoolhouse as a mischief rather than attending church with his family."

"The schoolhouse, up on the hill, out of reach of the water," I said. "But–" Suddenly I could not breathe, let alone speak.

"None of us knew Brian had survived. Not until you told us. Oh, some of the children still spoke of him occasionally, but no one believed them. You see, here in Conconully, it is still 1893, and it has been so for a very long time. I had thought it would always be so, until you arrived. I knew Oscar was still alive, even though I haven't seen him since before the flood, because of the goods he continues to bring for us. But young Brian's parents are still grieving him."

I found my voice. "But you said no one else survived. And it is not 1893, it is 1910." I stared at him. "You were the confidence man."

"Yes."

"Mr. Miller was the teamster."

Mr. Pepper nodded. "Yes. His widow still lives here."

"His wife? Has she seen him?"

"Alas, no."

"How did this *happen*?" I demanded.

He shook his head again. "I wish I knew. I would like to show you something, if you will come with me."

It was as if I had no mind of my own. Woodenly I followed him outside, down the lane to the main street, empty now in the starlight, the buildings merely shadows, their windows glinting. Were they broken? Was I back in a ghost town? I could not see well enough to tell. At last he stopped in front of the big blue community building and peered into its singularly dark bay windows. He sighed. "Well, perhaps not yet."

He turned to lead me back. I hesitated, but it would do no good not to ask. "What happened to Brian?"

"You will have to get him to tell you, I'm afraid."

"Will I see him again?"

"I hope so. He fell silent until we reached Belinda's house once more. He gestured me in. "Sleep well, Miss Ogden."

I doubted I would, after the story he'd told me. If it was true, and it did begin to explain what I had seen, even if it raised far more questions than it answered, then I was trapped in a town full of madmen. I merely shook my head and opened the door.

"You might talk with Sheriff Reilly," Mr. Pepper added as he turned away. "He and Doctor Duvall both arrived here after the flood, if not by their own free will as you did. You might find their stories illuminating."

I had no desire whatsoever for more stories. Not if they were like the nonsense I had just listened to.

"Good night, sir," I said, and shut the door behind me as if closing it against ghosts.

Mr. Pepper's story was both frightening and comforting to me, somehow. It was as if I had been expecting an explanation of some sort, but how could anyone expect a story that outlandish? But it felt as if I'd known all along I'd stumbled into something inexplicable. And it still was. But at least I could admit it was, even as I refused to believe a word of it.

I went to the bedroom and prepared for bed. I was quite sure sleep would not come, but I did not know what else to do. After I donned my night dress I went to the window and pulled back the curtain enough to look out.

The sky was clear, and the river of stars I had missed so much when I lived in Seattle arced across the heavens like the handle of Earth's basket. A sliver of new moon hung from it like an untied ribbon. I could not see the school from here, even in broad daylight; this window faced in the other direction, out to meadow and woods. I wondered what I would find if I did. Would the boy Brian have lit a lamp to chase away the dark? Or was he a shadow himself?

He was real. I knew it with every atom of my being. Mr. Pepper was real, too, and Belinda, and the schoolchildren, and every person I'd met here. I now found myself less sure of Mr. Miller, but everyone else, or at least Mr. Pepper, was laboring under a misconception, trying to hide something. Trying to *hide* something?

Mr. Pepper was, by his own admission, a confidence man, yet he expected me to believe a story so outlandish even P.T. Barnum would be hard pressed to accept it.

I let the curtain drop and turned to the bed. I would talk with the sheriff and the doctor tomorrow, if I must. But the questions I would ask would *not* be the ones Mr. Pepper expected.

CHAPTER 12

Oddly enough, I felt quite recovered the next morning, but Belinda, who came downstairs to find me frying eggs and buttering bread in the kitchen, was most welcome company, even if her primary emotion seemed to be one of relief. That I was well, or that I was still there at all?

I placed a plateful in front of her, and went to make more for myself. "I went ahead and made breakfast. I hope it's all right."

"Of course." She took up the pepper grinder, and I tried not to grimace. "What are your plans for this lovely Saturday?"

I stared at her. "Saturday?"

"Why, yes. Did you lose track?"

"I-I must have." I closed my mouth and scooped my eggs out of the pan in the nick of time. "I had hoped to talk with—" I paused. It might be easier to start with the little doctor. "Dr. Duvall."

Belinda set down her fork and frowned at me. "Are you feeling ill again? Come, sit down." This as I was already headed for the table, plate and coffee cup in hand.

"I am feeling fine. Quite well, actually. I— it was something Mr. Pepper said to me last night. He suggested I might ask Dr. Duvall about some questions I had."

To my surprise, Belinda did not ask me about my questions, or if perhaps she might help me with them. Instead she reached over and patted my hand where it lay on the table. The gesture warmed me. I was so fortunate to have had her take me in, and I knew it. I hoped she did not regret the impulse.

She was beginning to feel like a friend. Not in the same way Jean had, but then I could not imagine two people less alike. Jean was a go-getter, a mountain-mover, a woman out to prove herself in a world of men. Belinda was a seamstress, which was about as traditional a profession for a woman, if such an expression was not a contradiction in terms, as mine was as a schoolteacher. Jean belonged in the big city. Belinda was content in a small town.

Jean was forever dissatisfied and chasing ambition. Belinda knew what she could do and did it to the best of her ability, which was substantial.

Jean was unhappy. Belinda was – not. I had never considered where that choice left a person before.

"I'm sure she'll be able to," Belinda said.

"Be able to do what?" I asked, confused.

"Answer your questions," Belinda said confidently. "And," she added, her smile growing sly, "if she can't, I'm quite sure she'll come up with something."

"I am glad you're feeling better, and I'm sure Doctor Amy will be glad to see you for herself, as well." She rose and picked up her dishes. "I received a new barrel of cloth this week," from Mr. Miller's wagonload? I wondered, "and should finish going through it this morning. There was a piece of linen on top exactly the color of your eyes. Perhaps I could make it up for you?"

The color of a gloomy day? That would be cheerful. But she had gone on. "I was thinking of taking a walk through the woods this afternoon, and wondered if you would like to accompany me."

Through the woods? I blurted out the first thing to come to my mind, after Mr. Pepper's wild story and Dr. Duvall's warnings. "Is it safe?"

A shadow crossed her face, but she answered readily enough. "Oh, yes. We won't go far. But I love the woods and meadows in the springtime. We might even see some early wildflowers."

"All right," I found myself answering. "That would be lovely."

Belinda left not long afterward, telling me to come back home after I spoke with Dr. Duvall so she could show me the cloth, and she would have a picnic for us to take with us. It all sounded much better than what I was about to do, and I wished we could leave now so I could skip the conversation I did not want to have.

But something was pushing me, and I wanted, no, I needed for practical Doctor Amy to dispel the sense of utter unreality Mr. Pepper had spun last night. She, I was quite convinced, would set set things right.

Never mind it was what she and the sheriff had told me about Brian that I could not believe in the first place.

"It's good to see you so steady on your feet again," was the doctor's first assessment, made as I approached her.

We were on Conconully's main street, on the corner where it met what I had mentally dubbed School Street, but which turned out to be called Wauconda Avenue. She had apparently decided to come check on me, but had not seemed all that surprised to find me out and about.

I nodded, feeling a bit embarrassed, to be honest. "I don't know what came over me last night. I am not normally the vaporous type."

She laughed. "No, you look pretty solid to me."

I didn't quite know what to say to that. "I should hope so." I hesitated. "Mr. Pepper came by to visit me last night."

"I thought he might." She didn't say anything else, but fell into step beside me.

I steeled myself against her reaction. "He told me the most outlandish story."

She merely smiled. "I thought he might."

"He started out by telling me he was a confidence man, and then asked me to believe what I told him."

"A con man? Well, that's more than he's told me. Dan, too, I thnk. I wonder if the rest of the town knows." She didn't sound upset or angry, or even perturbed.

"He said to ask you about the year."

Her eyebrows flew up. She hesitated, then said, "I don't suppose–well, 1984."

I stared at her, speechless.

She laughed, apparently at my expression. "Don't ask Dan, then. Or, I suppose Max told you to." She stopped, and I with her. We were in front of the sheriff's office/house again. "Come on. Might as well get it all over with at once."

I followed her up the steps and across the little porch. Dr. Duvall knocked, then called out, "Hey, sleepyhead, you've got company. Rise and shine."

The door flew open. "Hold your horses. I wasn't asleep– Oh. Good morning, Miss Ogden."

"Max paid her a visit last night," Amy told him. "Gave her a story she can't believe."

Both of them seemed to find this vastly amusing. Sheriff Reilly gestured us both in. Amy, seemingly as at home here as in her own house, led the way to the parlor.

After we were seated, I said, fairly sure I didn't want to know, "Mr. Pepper told me I was to ask you about the year."

"Did he?" the sheriff asked, apparently a rhetorical question because he went on, "What would you say if I told you 2014?"

That, even more than Dr. Duvall's 1984, left me unable to say a single word.

"A hundred and twenty-one years from now, yup," he said, obviously mistaking my dumbfoundedness for an attempt at simple calculation. Which was wrong, of course. 2014 minus 1910 equaled ninety-four years, not a hundred and twenty-one.

I found my voice at last – it seemed to be deserting me at the most inopportune times – "What is the significance of these years so far into the future?"

"That's when we came from," Dr. Duvall said matter of factly.

I must have manifested some signs of fainting again, although I did not feel them, because she added abruptly, "Go fetch some tea, Dan."

I leaned back in my chair, grateful for the support. "Mis-Mister Pepper is not the only madman here?"

"Shh..." Dr. Duvall took my wrist and held it for a moment. Her fingers were cool and dry. "Your pulse is galloping."

I supposed it was. "I must leave–" leave this house, leave this accursed town, leave these people, leave this insanity –

"Claudia, you *can't*. If you do, you'll die. Dear God, I can't tell her *that*." This to the sheriff, who came in bearing an overflowing china cup.

"I think we're going to have to." But he sounded worried out of all proportion, too.

"Tell me what?" It was all I could do to say the words. Not more. Please not more, I thought rather wildly.

"Your friend?" The sheriff asked. "Jean? Miss Clancy?"

I was suddenly more than sure I did not want to hear the rest. The cup and saucer shook in my hand, the china chiming, the tea sloshing.

Dr. Duvall took it from me and set it on the low table in front of the sofa. "Your friend was here. She tried to leave. And it killed her.

I remember very little for some time after that. When I woke up again, I was back in my own comfortable bed, quilts piled over me. Beautifully made quilts, layered with tiny stitches in elaborate patterns. I fingered them, enjoying the colors and textures, pushing whatever it was that I would not remember at the back of my mind with a firm hand. Beautiful calicoes, striped and sprigged and patterned, sewn into intricate designs, the colors melding and combining into something so exquisite they looked like works of art.

I concentrated on the colors, the designs, the craftsmanship as hard as I could. It was the only way I could–

The door opened. It was too late for me to close my eyes and feign sleep. She'd already seen me. I cringed back. I could not help myself.

Belinda smiled at me. I could not smile back, and her expression became a bit stiff. She came forward and sat on the chair next to my bed. "Dr. Duvall had you brought home," she told me. "Since you weren't feeling as well as you thought you were. She said it might be a good idea to check on you every once in a while."

"Dr. Duvall does not want me left alone," I said flatly. "I'm sorry to be such trouble."

"It's no trouble. I think she would have stayed with you herself, but her life is not her own these days, what with the wedding and all. Unfortunately, you are not her only patient." She sounded careful, as if fearing to offend me. "But I am very glad to have you here." She frowned when I backed away, and pulled her hand back from where she had been reaching out toward me as well.

I knew I was being rude, but I realized I had another question. "What year did you come from?"

She looked puzzled for a moment, then her face cleared. "The year is 1893, Claudia," she said gently. She did reach out and touch my arm then, or tried to. I backed up still further and jerked my arm away, pulling those beautiful quilts up to cover myself.

"Not to me, it isn't. When I left Seattle, it was 1910."

She smiled. "Truly? You will have to tell me all about it when you are feeling better."

"You, you know?" I had so many questions I did not know where to begin asking. But another unwelcome thought occurred to me, and chased the others away. "Did-did you know my friend Jean Clancy?"

"Yes, I did." Her voice was sad, her tone telling me what she thought she knew even before she said the words. "She's gone, Claudia."

I stared at her. "Gone?" She wasn't here in Conconully, that I was well aware of. Surely Belinda wasn't trying to tell me she was *dead*. "What do you mean?"

Even sadder. "Max found her, out in the woods after she tried to leave."

But I had seen her, alive and well in Seattle, in 1910, a few days, weeks – not long ago, at any rate. I could not remember exactly how long, or when. I was beginning to wonder if I'd been dreaming everything that had led me here. Dazed, almost blinded with sudden dizziness, I managed, "Dead? But she can't be!"

She looked as if she wished she hadn't said anything at all, but she replied, "She is. I am so sorry, Claudia."

This time, when she leaned forward, not only to touch my arm but to take me into a warm embrace, I did not flinch back, but let her hold me as the tears I could not keep back flooded out. I could not escape this madness. I wept for grief, and for myself as well as Jean.

CHAPTER 13

I didn't know what to do, or who to be, or even if I wanted to exist, just for that moment. It was selfish of me, I suppose, but I in the short time since I'd met Jean and come to know her, she had become my best friend. My only friend in Seattle. I would not be here in Conconully, with a position and a home and new friends, except for her generosity. I had not realized how much I'd hoped she would come here, to find me, to visit me and her hometown, how I wanted to show her what her kindness had done for me. And now I couldn't. And would never be able to.

Eventually I drew back and took the handkerchief Belinda handed me. "I am sorry," I told her. "Belinda–" I inhaled deeply and blew my nose a second time. "Why didn't anyone tell me before now?"

She sighed. "I don't know about the others. I wished not to be the one to cause you pain. But I see I only made things worse by my actions. So it is I who needs to apologize to you, not the other way round." Her tone became earnest, and her voice a bit strained. "Can you forgive me?"

Her hand still rested on mine. It felt warm and comforting, like that of a friend. Well, and she *was* my friend. It felt almost like a betrayal, to think of Belinda as a friend when Jean was, was dead. And Belinda had kept the knowledge from me. How could I feel she was a friend, how could I feel anything toward- toward someone who had kept something like that from me, that I'd had a right to know. Her only misstep had been out of concern for me.

It was a horrible thing to think, let alone to say, and I would *not* say it. But I would say, and mean it, to Belinda, that she had my forgiveness, even though I did not believe she needed it.

"You did the right thing. I wasn't ready to hear such news when I first arrived here, nor would I have believed you then. Any of you," I added hastily.

"Do you believe me now?" she asked.

I thought about it for a moment. "I shouldn't. After everything else I've been told since I arrived here, I shouldn't believe anything."

"But you do." She sounded relieved. "I know it's selfish of me to ask, but does this mean you will stay?"

"Where else would I go?" I asked wryly.

Somehow I was not surprised to see Mr. Pepper standing in the doorway, but it did not keep me from pulling the covers up to my chin. Belinda, too, let go of my hand and sat back in her chair, but not before the little man's curious eyes saw the gesture. His eyebrows rose, but he smiled – no, he smirked. All he said, however, was, "It's always your choice, Miss Ogden."

He stepped further into the room. "I am glad to see you're feeling better."

"Maximilian Pepper," Belinda said, sounding every bit as indignant as I felt, "Leave this room this instant."

"Yes, ma'am." And he left, leaving me wondering why I felt as if he'd been there only to issue his odd proclamation.

"That man has no manners," Belinda said, shaking her head. "Would you like me to bring you breakfast, or do you feel able to get up?"

"Oh, my," I said, a laugh escaping me in spite of myself, in spite of Jean, in spite of everything. It was as if I could not help it. And as if– Jean had often told me to stop behaving like Atlas, with the weight of the world on my shoulders. Perhaps it was time I took her up on her advice. In her memory. "Such decadence. I can get up. I'd like to get up."

Belinda beamed at me so brightly she made me blink. "In that case, I have something for you."

The something turned out to be a new shirtwaist and skirt. The style was a bit old-fashioned. I am no fashion historian, but I suspected the outfit would have been quite at home on my mother when I was a child. But the fabrics were lovely and the tailoring exquisite. I fingered the row of tucks down the front of the waist and said, "I can't take this. It's too much."

"Consider it part of your salary as teacher," Belinda replied. "As well as your room and board." She closed her mouth and, inexplicably, blushed.

"You have no children," I said.

"No, but others do, and they pay me in kind as well. That is how things work here."

No salary? Well, it wasn't as if I needed for anything. My salary in Seattle had not allowed for anything beyond the bare necessities and the occasional bit I sent to Montana to help the family and expiate my guilt over having left them. I suspected I would not be able to do that from here–

I should not have felt relieved. I should not have been happy I was no longer able to fulfill an obligation I had long since begun to resent.

"Here, let me help you," Belinda said, and held out a hand.

I gave her mine, and let her help me dress. Her hands were gentle as she fastened buttons and straightened my collar and brushed my hair for me. I could not help feeling cared for. Oddly enough, Belinda's actions reminded me of Jean's when she'd arranged my life, packing me up and putting me on the train, giving me my handful of tickets. It was as if I meant something to her.

She tucked a last pin into my bun and stood back. "There. A neat-as-a-pin schoolteacher."

I glanced down ruefully. "I never owned such pretty clothing as a schoolteacher in Seattle."

Her smile broadened into a grin. "Perhaps, then, you *should* stay."

I nodded. "Perhaps I should."

We did go for a walk that afternoon, after I convinced Belinda that I was able by insisting I cook our luncheon. We wandered down along the little stream out of town, in a different direction from the one I had arrived. The road narrowed down from the wide, hard-packed main street, to two narrow ruts running side by side in the green grass, knee-deep and brushing against our skirts. Birds chirped and butterflies coasted from wildflower to wildflower of every description. I wondered if it was spring on the other side of the mountains, or if it would be spring at all anywhere else but here.

I had made a hobby as a child of learning the names of flowers, and amused Belinda more than I realized I had when I glanced up from admiring an eschscholzia, or California poppy, to find her watching me with an expression that made my stomach feel odd. Not ill, but–

"I see why you became a teacher," she said.

I shrugged helplessly. "I enjoy beauty more when I can call it by name."

"It is a lovely shade of orange," she agreed. "On a flower, that is. I would not care to make an entire dress out of that color."

"I'm afraid in that quantity one would look a bit like a pumpkin."

She laughed, and I with her. It was a relief simply to laugh, and to be. To not think about Seattle, and my position, my former position, that is, or my family back in Montana, who could not send me letters here demanding I come home. Most of all, not to think about Jean, who was gone forever.

"Look over here," I said, and impulsively I grasped Belinda's hand. She did not draw back as Jean had on the few occasions I had done so to her, but let me draw her down to observe a mariposa lily, the dark spots on its white petals gleaming like rich velvet. She stayed crouched beside me as we discussed the other flowers near it.

And when we stood, and I reluctantly made to let go, she held on for a moment longer, and, to my delight, we strolled hand in hand across the sunny meadow. I had never spent so pleasant an afternoon. I would not feel guilty about that. I would not.

"Of course you will come to church," Belinda told me firmly on our way back.

I sighed. "I know. I'm expected. The children's parents will want proof the teacher is a God-fearing woman." I had never felt welcome in church. My parents' church had never made me feel at home even as a child, and one part of living in Seattle I had appreciated was the fact that no one paid any attention to my attendance at religious services. Seattle had enough churches that, even had I been asked, I could have told those of one church I went to another and so forth and so on, without ever having been caught.

But in a small town like Conconully, I could not manage such sleight of hand.

Belinda gave me an odd look. "It is none of my business, of course
—"

A shadow darted between one building and the next. A blond,
tousle-haired shadow in ragged clothing. "Excuse me," I said, picked up
my new skirt, and darted after it.

He led me a merry chase, and when I at last caught up to him, I
was panting myself. I could feel my hair trickling down from the neat
bun Belinda had constructed for me. "Brian Whittaker, where have
you been?" I panted. I grasped his arm as he made to duck behind the
building. The schoolhouse? Yes, I had run clear up the hill after him.
No wonder I was out of breath.

"H-hello, Teacher." He sounded nervous, his arm thin beneath my
hand. Criminally thin. *He* was not out of breath, but then he was young
and undoubtedly spent a great deal of his time being a slippery fish.
"Did you want me?" He stared down at where I hung onto him as if —
as if I thought he might disappear. Again. And so I did. "That hurts."

"Will you promise not to run if I let go of you?"

"I-I can't." He looked as if he were about to cry. "Please. Let go."

The situation was untenable. I lifted my hand. He stood still.

"I only want to help. I thought you would run again."

"No." I could see his thin chest rise and fall. "Not now. I'm sorry."

I knelt down in front of him, my hem dragging in the dust. If the
slight damage hurt Belinda's feelings I would apologize later, but some
things are more important. "I'm sorry I hurt you. I do only want to
help you." I wasn't sure I should say what I needed to tell him next, but
he needed to know. "Your parents miss you. They're grieving for you,
because they think you're dead."

A tear welled up and overflowed to trail down his cheek. He swiped
at it and gulped, as if he thought he should be a man and not cry. "I
know, Teacher."

"Why don't you go to them, then? They would be overjoyed to see you, and I'm sure they'd forgive whatever it was you did that made you run away."

"I don't know how." It was the most desolate thing I'd ever heard a child say.

Right then, Belinda came puffing up the hill. "Claudia, whatever is the matter?"

I looked from her, to the boy Brian. He was gone.

I am still not sure why I should have been surprised it was so, or of my new reluctance to speak of the boy to Belinda. I suspected she would think me mad, or that I was trying to make light of our friendship by lying to her.

"Nothing," I said at last. "I thought I saw something, but I was mistaken."

"I heard you speak to someone," she said, sounding troubled.

And now I was trapped. Either way I would lose her respect. All I could do was deny it. "I did not say anything."

And that, it turned out, was the worst choice of all. Her face went still and her posture stiffened. Without a word, she started back down the hill. I followed her, thinking, no, what I meant to say is I was speaking with a child everyone else thinks is dead, but I didn't want to tell you because I didn't want you to think I'm crazy.

But I could not say it. When we reached the house, she did not go in the front door, but went around to the side, to the separate entrance to her workroom. I followed her, but before I could reach it, she had closed the door firmly behind her. I tried the handle, anyway. It was locked.

Slowly I made my way back around the house to the front, the dry grasses sweeping against my skirt, avoiding the loose boards of the porch when I made my way up the step. I opened the creaking door and went into the parlor, which this morning had been bright and clean and shining. It was now covered with dust and festooned with cobwebs. It was as if no one had set foot in here in a dozen years.

The door from the parlor to Belinda's workroom was locked as well, and she did not respond to either my voice or my knocks. Finally, I gave up and spent what remained of the day trying to repair the worst of the neglect. She did not respond to calls for supper, either. I fell on the musty-smelling mattress long after dark. At least I was tired enough to fall asleep as soon as my head hit the pillow.

I woke to a bedroom smelling – and appearing – much cleaner than it had the night before. The chair in the corner no longer boasted a hole in its upholstery, where I had found and evicted a family of mice the night before. The wallpaper was firmly attached to the walls and not peeling in strips, and the rug was whole.

It was as if I had dreamed the whole thing in a nightmare. Perhaps I had. I could hear the church bell ringing even from here, and I had no idea how late I was.

I pulled on a dress I found in my wardrobe, another with Belinda's unmistakably fine stitches. It was lovely, of course, a sprigged lawn I would never have chosen for myself as a spinster schoolteacher, and I grimaced as I fastened the buttons. I did hope my students' parents would not think me too frivolous when they saw me in it, but I was quite sure they would approve even less of anything else I had to choose from.

It certainly was not appropriate for mourning, but that could not be helped, either.

Belinda was nowhere to be found. I hurried down to Conconully's main road and saw I was not late, to my relief. Streams of people, all in their Sunday best, were making their way to a white building, its steeple taller than I would have expected silhouetted against a bright blue sky.

All of the young faces I saw when I entered the church were familiar, although I looked in vain for the boy Brian. As were a few of the grown-up ones. Amy and Dan waved at me but moved on, and the Missels nodded at me in greeting.

I thought I caught a glimpse of Belinda, her back to me as she entered the church, and my suspicion was confirmed when she seated herself then turned back, as if looking for someone. Not me. Surely not me.

But I could tell the instant she saw whoever it was she was looking for, because her face broke out into a smile that made me catch my breath, and she gestured for someone to join her. Someone? I could not believe it, but she was smiling and gesturing at me.

I squared my shoulders and made my way up the aisle, hoping I was not wrong and no one else would reach that inviting empty space next to her on the pew before I did.

Smiles surrounded me as people chatted and welcomed each other. Several times I was stopped to say hello to one of my young pupils and be breathlessly introduced to the child's parents.

But at last I reached the pew where Belinda sat, the empty space next to her miraculously still there. "Is anyone sitting here?" I asked, hoping against hope that she was not holding the space for someone else, that she had forgiven me.

"I believe you are," she told me. "I am so glad you found the dress."

I could not help but smile. "Not too frivolous for a teacher?"

I could have bitten my tongue but her smile only broadened. "There are no laws stating a teacher may not be a bit frivolous in her dress outside of the classroom. It's lovely on you."

I sat, taking care with my beautiful skirts. The church was quieting down, people seating themselves. At last, the only sound to be heard was the ringing bell above us, and then it stopped, too, leaving a peaceful, anticipatory hush. I let out my breath and quelled an urge to reach out for Belinda's hand, only to feel hers reach for mine. I glanced down in surprise, but our skirts covered our misdemeanor, and I squeezed her fingers lightly. She smiled, looking up at the pulpit, and so did I.

CHAPTER 14

All around me I felt the press of people, there because they wanted to be, because they believed in God, in spite of who they were or what had happened to them. In spite of being in a place I could only think of as being out of time. The oddest thought occurred to me. Was this heaven, this little mining town in the middle of nowhere? Was this the afterlife promised in the Bible? I stifled a giggle, and felt Belinda's fingers press on mine. I pressed back.

I would not make of myself any more of a spectacle than I felt already, nor jeopardize my new position, which I was already beginning to value.

But as a young man I did not recognize took to the pulpit to lead us all in a hymn, I sang along with everyone else, wondering if that was the reason why both Amy and Belinda had asked me about my happiness since I'd arrived.

And if this was heaven, why had I not died to get here?

I gulped mid-stanza, my throat suddenly dry, and could not produce a single note more. Belinda glanced over at me, her expression concerned. I nodded at her and began to mouth the words. She gave me a baffled look, but then turned her attention back to the young choir master and I let out my breath in relief.

The hymn ended at last and we all reseated ourselves. I was grateful for the hard wooden pew, for the back and the end of it which supported me as well. At the moment I felt as if they were all that was keeping me upright.

"Are you ill?" Belinda whispered, her breath soft on my ear.

"No, I'm fine. I had a thought, was all." And had I ever.

She said no more, but settled back next to me.

The redoubtable Mr. Pepper approached the pulpit, and I could feel my eyes widen. He was the pastor? Not exactly the religious sort, I would have thought, let alone religious enough to study for a minister.

But he smiled down benevolently at us all, Bible in hand, and said, to my horror, "Today we have a new believer among us, for the first time in too long. Please, after the service, welcome our new schoolteacher, Miss Claudia Ogden."

I felt as if every eye in the building turned upon me, and not in a pleasant way. Curiosity is one thing, and it is to be encouraged in one's students, but at this moment I felt as if they wished to dissect me, their inquisitiveness was so great.

Even after Mr. Pepper went on to the rest of the service, I could feel gazes burning on me, as if they hadn't seen anyone like me ever before. For all I knew, they hadn't.

"Today's text," said Mr. Pepper, "is one we all need to remember. It comes from the book of John, chapter fourteen, verse one. 'Let not your heart be troubled: ye believe in God, believe also in me.'"

He preached on with the voice of a natural orator. As he spoke, his gaze scanned the congregation – why did I want to think of them as his audience instead? – never lighting on me, for which I was grateful.

Yes, my heart was troubled. It had been for a very long time, and now, having learned of Jean's death, it was more troubled still. How had I arrived in this place out of time? Did it mean that I, and all of these people, were not alive to the outside world? Or were they all playing an elaborate game with me? Should I believe anything they told me?

And, suddenly, Jean's death felt real again, and this place felt real, and perhaps I was the one who was not. I stifled a sob, earning another concerned glance from Belinda. I shook my head and bowed it. Fortunately for me at that moment, so did everyone else. Mr. Pepper had ended his sermon with a prayer.

The young choir director took the pulpit again and led the congregation in another hymn. Afterward, everyone began to file out of the pews and down the aisle, the end of the service releasing voices so the sanctuary hummed again with chatter.

It took far longer than I would have liked for the two of us to make our way down the aisle and out the double doors to the spring-dappled street. I could not resent the enveloping welcome, but it was almost more than I could stand.

I watched myself shake hands and smile and nod, as if I had no control, as if my body knew what needed to be done without paying the least bit of attention to my mind.

That was, until a couple about my age stepped forward. Theirs was not the uncomplicated welcome of Mr. Pepper's other parishioners, but a complex mix of fear and longing even I could read like a primer. I did not wish to speak to these people. I knew this beyond the shadow of a doubt. I glanced over at Belinda, who was frowning, but she shrugged, helplessly, I thought.

"Miss— Ogden, is it?" The man asked. He was, as I have said, about my age, dressed in a black suit in the same old-fashioned style everyone wore here. His hair was blond, the same shade as the boy Brian's, I thought against my will. His wife, clinging to his arm, was short and slight, in a dress obviously dyed black for mourning.

"Yes." I did not ask which of my pupils belonged to them.

He hesitated briefly. "I am George Whittaker, and this is my wife Theresa. We are – were – Brian's parents."

I heard Belinda's indrawn breath beside me, or perhaps it was my own. I could not say anything at first, or what was I *to* say? I am sorry for your loss made no sense whatsoever even though it was obvious they thought their child was dead. Demanding of them why they had abandoned their son, whom they obviously loved, would be outright cruelty.

Before I managed to choose words, Mr. Pepper bustled up. "Now, George, Theresa, now is not the time."

Mr. Whittaker turned on him, and both of them took those searching gazes from me to Mr. Pepper. "And when is a good time, Max?" His voice rose above the remaining babble.

Belinda was tugging at my sleeve. "Come along."

"But-but—"

"Max will take care of them. Their grief is still too new." She pulled me along beside her, past several groups of curious onlookers, into the street.

I could not help glancing back as we strode along, to see Mrs. Whittaker looking at me with a longing I could not bear. I picked up the pace until Belinda had to lengthen her stride to keep up with me. "Why are they grieving for the child they abandoned?" I could not help asking.

Belinda merely shook her head.

"They *did* abandon him. It's a marvel he has survived."

Still no answer.

If he is any example of how this town treats misfits—" I thought of Jean and how like a misfit she must have felt here. Of how I had flashes of feeling like I belonged, only to have them snatched away in mystery almost as soon as they – manifested?

"Belinda?"

But we had arrived at our house. She finally looked at me straight on. "I don't know, Claudia. I simply don't know." Then she turned on her heel and went to her bedroom.

After an awkward lunch I spent the afternoon alone, trying to treat Sunday as it should be treated. In my parents' house in Montana, Sunday was a day different from every other, to be treated with reverence. I remembered sitting in the parlor, the tick of the clock the loudest noise in the room, the turn of the pages of my father's Bible a whisper like voices heard from far away.

Sometimes he read aloud in a low voice I had to strain to hear, so different from his workaday speech, almost always from Paul or the Old Testament. About how who we were supposed to be, not about love. Not like the verse Mr. Pepper had expounded upon this morning.

This afternoon I was the one with a Bible in my hand, and there was no clock, nor anyone else to read aloud to. I wished I had been able to hold onto the boy Brian, that he was here, filling his stomach and listening to me read aloud to him. I wished Belinda was with me, too, that she sat with her lap full of sewing and her lovely smile on her face.

I did not dare to go to her. I would have gone searching for Brian, but somehow I knew *trying* to find him would only chase him further away. He knew where I was, and that I would treat him kindly if he arrived at my door. I could not force him to come to me. He had to come of his own free will.

He had to come, so I could show him it was a good thing for him to do.

The Bible, one I had found in the bookcase, fell from my loose hands. I could not concentrate, or pay even enough attention for the words in front of me to register. I caught it before it slipped from my lap to the floor and set it aside. I needed to sleep. I needed– something. I had, I thought drowsily, leaning my head against the high back of the upholstered chair, never felt quite this odd before in my entire life.

I woke to familiar voices.

"–like this, Doc Amy," Belinda said in a worried tone. "Surely this can't be right."

A gusty sigh. "This case is outside my experience. Obviously, the illness that brought her here was trying to kill her, but without diagnostic tests I can't tell you whether it's worse or better or what. She says she was dying before she arrived here, and I think that's why she's able to stay. But after what happened to Alan Arngrim last winter, I don't trust my gut on that one anymore."

I opened my eyes. I was still in the big upholstered wing chair. Doctor Amy was seated on the ottoman in front of me. She appeared to hold one of my hands in hers, her fingers pressed to my wrist, but oddly I could not feel them. Belinda was out of my line of sight. Moving my head to find her did not seem like a good idea to me then.

"She won't die here too, will she?"

"Shh, she's awake. Claudia, can you hear me?"

I tried to answer verbally. I tried to nod. I suddenly realized I could do neither and panic filled me. I could feel my eyes widen, though, and knew the instant the young doctor saw they had.

"It's all right, Claudia. At least I hope it is. Can you blink?"

I hoped I could. I tried. Apparently I succeeded, because Amy smiled at me, obviously relieved. "Well, it's plain you can hear me, but do me a favor and confirm it, will you? Blink twice for me if you can hear me."

I did so.

"Well, that's good news." Her tone changed utterly. "How did that cat get in?"

I blinked again, not knowing how – what cat?

"Captain," Belinda said, and suddenly a weight pushed down on my lap, a real weight. Sharp claws kneaded my lap through my skirt, pinpricks on my skin I *could* feel, and suddenly I could feel Amy's hand as well. Belinda came into my line of sight, intent on removing the cat. "Captain, get down."

"No," I said firmly. I'm not sure who was more surprised, me, Amy, who after a second grinned broadly, or Belinda, who frowned.

"He'll pull threads in the fabric," she said, sounding as if she thought she should disapprove but couldn't quite bring herself to.

I brought my hand up to the cat's sleek fur. "He's not hurting anything. Where did he come from?"

"Well, that was a quick recovery," Amy said. "I'll have to remember to bring a cat along every time someone gets sick. All joking aside, though, do you realize you weren't breathing when Belinda found you here?"

I gazed at her in startlement, my hand gone still. The cat head-butted at it in protest. "Not breathing? How is it I'm still alive?"

"Good question." Amy glanced over at Belinda, whose fingers covered her mouth and whose eyes were wide. "Could you make us some tea? Peppermint? If you don't have any, there's some dried in my office, in the far left jar on the top shelf. I think it might be just the thing."

"Of course." Belinda left without hesitation.

"Peppermint?" It was not one of my favorites, but if the doctor thought that was what I needed, I supposed I could choke it down.

"I keep some around for stomach ailments. But," as I began to tell her my stomach was fine, "it was the first thing that came to mind to get her out of here for a bit.

"We need to talk."

CHAPTER 15

"All right," I said slowly. I was not at all sure I wished to have this discussion, but I knew the choice wasn't mine.

"How have you been feeling? Before this afternoon, that is?"

I tried to give it some thought. "Quite well, actually."

"Have you been in any kind of pain?"

"Only what is normal." I gestured, awkwardly, but she nodded understanding, to my great relief.

"Oh, cramps?" She smiled. "You had me worried there. Although–exactly how bad are these cramps and how often have you had them since you've been here?"

She chatted about bodily functions as if they were proper topics for discussion. I wished I could sink through the floor, but she would want an honest answer. "I-I had them almost all the time, before I came here. Sometimes worse than others, but they never really went away. And," I added, surprised, "no, I have not had them since I arrived here. How odd."

"How odd indeed," Amy said, echoing me. "Well, I'm going to ask you something that might upset you, something I'd like to do."

I was not sure how I could be more embarrassed. I steeled myself. "Go ahead."

"I'd like to palpitate your abdomen. See if I can feel anything – unusual about your female organs. What I'd really like to do is give you a pelvic exam and a pap smear, but the first is probably more invasive than you'd stand for, and the second, well, I don't have the kit or the lab to send the results to. Not to mention that I never had the training."

I stared at her in confusion. She laughed wryly. "I know. I really don't think whatever made you sick made it this far, anyway, but I'd like to see if it did. Would you let me examine you? It would set my mind at ease, and it might do the same for you."

I nodded, and she had me lie down on my bed. When she was done, I know I was scarlet, but she seemed satisfied. More than satisfied. Pleased.

"Well, everything feels perfectly normal. Let me know if the cramps come back when you aren't actually menstruating, or if they get bad when you are. Otherwise, I think that part of you, at least, is quite healthy."

Just then, Belinda bustled back in, without tea, I noticed. "Amy Melissa Duvall," she announced, sounding more than a bit offended, "there is no tea of any kind in that bird's nest of an office of yours."

She saw me lying on the bed and added, in a completely different tone, "Oh, dear." She strode over to me and perched on the edge of the bed, taking my hands in hers. "Is it worse again?"

I sat up, seeing Amy slip out of the room out of the corner of my eye. "No. Doc Amy wished to - examine me. She found nothing wrong." I hesitated. "She seems to think I left my illness behind when I came here." This made no sense, or no less sense, than anything else which had happened to me since I'd met Mr. Miller in Omak. "She seems to think it's just taking time to heal. Whatever it was," I added helplessly.

134

Belinda grimaced. "Our Doc Amy means well, and while I understand she has some newfangled ideas, I can't say I've heard good things about them." She paused. "No, I can't say I've heard good things about her methods, at least while the speaker was still undergoing her treatments. But they've worked more often than not, which is more than I can say about old Doc Stark, most of the time."

"Doc Stark?"

She hesitated. "He used to be the doctor here, but he's gone now."

I stared at her in shock. "He *left*? How?"

Her hesitation this time was longer. "No, not left." Oh, I thought, and did not press her for details. Perhaps she and Dr. Stark had been friends. Perhaps she still mourned him. But then she smiled. "We were real glad when Dr. Duvall showed up. There's perfectly good tea in the kitchen, by the way. Come along."

"I worry about you," Belinda said as she poured the tea, *not* peppermint from the scent of it, thank goodness. "Finding you this afternoon scared ten years off of my life."

I opened my mouth, then closed it again as she set my cup and saucer in front of me.

She smiled at me as she slid the sugar bowl toward me. "I know you don't usually take sweetening, but you look like you could use the energy."

I found myself spooning sugar into the steaming hot tea, almost against my will. "How *do* I look?"

Belinda closed her eyes briefly, then stared at her cup as she stirred her own unadulterated tea. "I thought you were gone," she told me, her voice strained. "I thought you had faded away, and – you just got here."

It was an odd way to describe death, but not the first time I'd heard someone use that term here.

But she was still speaking. "But you weren't fading. You were just *there*, not breathing. It was like poor Mr. Arngrim last winter, but – nothing was *wrong* with you. *He'd* been injured–" She set her cup down, rattling in its saucer.

I put my hand on hers, sitting limply on the table. "I'm all right, Belinda. And I am sorry for your loss."

She nodded as if steadying herself. "I think, in his way, he was making way for your arrival. You're the first person we've had arrive here since the flood who came here of her own free will."

I stared at her, but she shook her head, then turned her hand over and clasped mine. "I never thought to be grateful to him," she told me. "But I am."

I took stock of myself as I prepared for a day in the classroom the following morning. So far as I could tell, my – faint, was the only thing I could think to call it – yesterday afternoon had been nothing more than an aberration. I felt well, as I had not felt since before I'd left Montana. I almost felt as if I had never been alive up until I'd come to Conconully.

Conconully, too, seemed more alive and vibrant and *real* than it had since I had arrived here. People smiled and nodded to me as I walked to school that morning, as if they were glad I was here. The buildings were bright and shiny, windows whole and all in good repair. Paint gleamed as if applied only yesterday. The commercial buildings, beginning to open this early in the morning, looked prosperous and sturdy.

I approached a large building painted blue with two huge bay windows, empty but for one odd thing, a statue of a pig. It looked as if it was made from plaster, and it stood proudly on the wide shelf behind one of the windows, as if surveying its domain.

I could not help but stop and stare back at it. Why did I have the very strong impression that it – he? – approved of me? It was not alive. It could not 'approve' of anything.

A moment later, I became aware of booted footsteps approaching me. With an effort, I turned away from the pig to see who it was, and the sheriff raised a hand in greeting. "Good morning," he said, and stopped abruptly, staring into the window as if as mesmerized by that silly plaster pig as I was. He glanced from the pig to me and back to the pig. "Harry's back. Well."

"Harry?" I could not help asking.

He looked sheepish, but he waved a hand at the pig. "Harry, Claudia. Claudia, Harry. Well, that's a good sign." Having made the ridiculous – introduction? he strode off, looking pleased for no reason I could see. The sun poked above the maple trees behind me. Oh, dear, I thought, I don't want to be late. I had work to do before my students arrived.

The pig, and the sheriff, along with our most peculiar conversation, fell from my thoughts as I strode up the hill to the schoolhouse. Early as it was still, a familiar small figure sat on the stoop. I could tell when he spotted me, because he sprang to his feet, looking as if he could not decide between greeting me or fleeing.

"Brian!" I exclaimed before he could do the latter. "I am so glad to see you. Where have you been?"

He gave me a sheepish look. "You're not angry with me, Teacher?"

"No, of course not. Just worried." I opened the door. "Come in. I brought you something." I had made up a parcel containing some meat and bread and some early strawberries, in hopes the boy Brian would turn up for school. I was glad I had as his eyes went wide when I pulled it out of my satchel. "Here. This is for you."

"Thank you, Teacher!" He fell upon the food as if he hadn't eaten for days, and my guilt at not pursuing him the day before was assuaged, slightly.

"Where have you been?" I asked him again.

He did not look up. "Around," he said vaguely around a mouthful. "You needn't worry about me."

"Where do you sleep?"

He did look at me then. "Sleep?"

"You must sleep somewhere." I wanted to take him to his parents this very minute, but I knew he would not go. Then another thought occurred to me, one I did not like at all. "Brian, do you know what fading is?"

He looked startled, then nodded. "I guess."

"Are *you* fading, Brian?"

He looked down at himself, then touched his face, as if he hadn't expected it to be there. "No. I don't think I am."

It was hardly a satisfactory answer, but I could hear the voices of the other children getting closer as they came up the hill. Brian had, too, I could tell.

"Thank you for the breakfast, Teacher," he said, and slipped away from me to his seat back in the corner.

Before I could say anything else, the children came clattering in. I watched as they seated themselves and settled down, to see if any of them did speak to Brian, but so far as I could tell they did not. He looked as if he wished he could, but he did not, either.

I called the room to order, and our day began.

He was still there at noon. This surprised me, as I assumed he would slip away as he had before, before I could offer what he obviously saw as unwelcome charity. Odd, that he would take food from me but no other help.

I didn't dare suggest we go to his parents yet, but perhaps— "I want you to come back to the house with me for lunch," I told him.

"No, thank you." His polite refusal belied the expression on his face. Who had told him he was not worth simple caring, or *was* it misplaced pride?

"I insist. Miss Houseman will have made more than enough, and I–"

"No, Teacher. She'll think you're loco." And he dashed out the door before I could catch him.

Loco? I'd run up against those who thought I was foolhardy to try to help the needier of my students before before, but crazy? I determined two things then and there. One, if food was all the boy would accept from me for now, then he would receive three square meals' worth from me every day until I could persuade him to go home to his parents. And two, I would get the boy's story from him if I had to pry it from him with a lever.

Belinda was not at the house when I arrived back there for lunch. She was not in her workshop, either. A note on the kitchen table apologized for her absence, but did not explain where she had gone.

She did not owe me an explanation. I was a bit disappointed to have missed her, but the note did say she would see me that evening. At any rate, I did not have to explain why, instead of fixing a meal from last night's leftovers, as her note suggested, I made enough sandwiches to satisfy two appetites and packed them back up to the schoolhouse to eat there.

But, as had happened before, Brian did not attend classes that afternoon. I left the food on his desk after the rest of my students were gone for the day, in hopes that he would return and find it, and strolled slowly back down the hill, watching my surroundings carefully.

"Looking for something?"

I jumped, but it was only Mr. Pepper. "Just one of my students. He skipped classes this afternoon and I wish to know why."

The little man tilted his head at me. "Who?"

I opened my mouth and closed it again, unsure what he would think of me should I answer him truthfully. Did Brian's "she'll think you're loco" apply to Mr. Pepper, too?

"Was it young Brian?"

I sighed. Then again, I should have realized he'd know. Mr. Pepper seemed to know far more than was possible. "Yes."

He fell in step beside me. "We all thought he was dead," he said in a companionable voice.

"Yes, I know," I told him tartly. "He is not."

"Do you know you're the only adult who can see him? He has a younger sister, but no one believed her when she insisted he was still alive. I don't know if she still believes she can or not. None of the other children will corroborate her story, either, although I am not sure they were telling the truth when they denied they'd seen him."

I stopped again, staring at him. "What do you mean, sir?" Surely he meant I was the only adult who acknowledged the child's existence, that a little boy was living among them while they ignored a child who told them otherwise, collectively pretending he was not there, barely subsisting. Why, I could not tell, but it certainly did not speak well of anyone here.

"I mean it quite literally," he said, sounding sad. "And I would like that to change, if we can manage it."

So, perhaps I had shamed him and the townsfolk into doing something about this disgraceful situation. Even if they were denying his existence to salve their feelings. Why didn't matter nearly as much as did what. "What can I do?"

"I don't know yet. But here we are. I am glad you have found somewhere to belong." We were, quite without my realizing it, standing in front of my new home. I wondered if he expected me to invite him in to continue our conversation. "I'm glad for you."

Not that I was about to. But Mr. Pepper was already tipping his hat to me and bowing himself away.

Then he turned back to look at me. "I hear Harry is back. I am glad of that as well."

Harry? Who? Then I remembered my odd encounter with the sheriff that morning. These people set more importance on a plaster pig than on a living child. I would change that, if it was the last thing I ever did.

But when I asked Belinda about the Whittakers' daughter, she only gave me an odd look, and asked if the little girl had been attending school. When I told her no, she said it was as well, as she'd heard the child was touched, a term I had not heard since my mother had used it to describe my grandfather. Touched by whiskey, I'd gathered as I grew older, although I knew the term covered a multitude of sins, as my mother would have said.

Belinda then changed the subject as deftly as she could turn a seam, telling me about the round she'd gone this afternoon with Althea Grayson, who had to have every stitch on her body just so, and who had been used to getting her clothing from a seamstress in Chicago.

"She was visiting her younger sister here when the flood happened. Trying to talk the poor girl, who's madly in love with her husband, to come back to Chicago and live under her thumb again. Poor Lisa had to elope to get away the first time, and now they're stuck together."

I drew back. "So not everyone's happy here?" But now that I thought about it, thought about the Whittakers—

"No." Belinda gave a wry chuckle. "Although some, like Althea, enjoy their discontent so much I do wonder if she and hers would be happy without anything to complain about. But she does have exquisite taste, and the wherewithal to pay for it." She hesitated. "Some have had poor favors from the Lord."

"Like Brian Whittaker's parents?" I could not help but ask.

"Yes."

"With no hope?"

Belinda raised her eyebrows at me. "Is that what you want? To give them hope?"

I was beginning to wonder when it was that I'd begun to feel so a part of this place – and these people – I barely knew. "Yes," I said firmly, with more confidence than I actually possessed.

"Perhaps," she said slowly, "that's why you've come here."

"What on earth do you mean?"

"Everyone needs a purpose, don't they?"

"I suppose."

But she nodded firmly at me, as if explaining everything. "I came here to because the town needed a seamstress. Doctor Amy came because Doc Stark left. Sheriff Reilly came because–"

"The town needed a policeman?" I finished her sentence for her.

Her lips curved. "Some didn't think so. But he's been good for us. And good for Doctor Amy."

"Do you believe what Doc Amy and the sheriff say about when they came from?" I asked abruptly.

I could see the disquiet in her eyes, but she answered me readily enough. "I believe they do. Ours is not to question, I don't think."

"Do you believe me?" It was suddenly very important.

She sighed, but her answer was not what I expected. "I wish I could see where you came from."

"I could show you."

I wished I could have bitten my tongue instead, when her back went stiff. "No one is going anywhere this evening. Have you eaten?"

In for a penny. "No. Neither has Brian, I'd wager." I almost stopped myself from taking a deep breath, and realized suddenly that I no longer had to constrain myself physically, because I was no longer in pain. The habit was so ingrained in me that I had continued to my careful habits even now, even though I hadn't been in pain for weeks. I could stand straight and breathe without constraint now. My abdomen did not feel swollen. The sensation, or lack of it, was so strong I completely forgot what I was about to say. I stood on tiptoe and stretched, reaching my fingertips almost to the low ceiling. I lowered my arms, spreading them out, and twirled like a ballerina I had seen in a book once, barely missing Belinda as she stepped back.

She was staring at me. But as I dropped back to a normal stance, my arms sinking to my sides, she smiled at me. "I do believe you're feeling better, aren't you?"

"It's so wonderful not to *hurt*," I told her, still not prepared to believe the evidence of my own senses. "I do think if you wanted me to be happy, if you could take the pain away forever, I'd promise to be happy for the rest of my life."

Now she was beaming. "Max told me Harry was back. I couldn't believe it then, but perhaps he was right."

I blinked. "I beg your pardon?"

But she wasn't paying attention. "This calls for a celebration. I'll send someone for Audrey, or we'll never hear the end of it."

CHAPTER 16

She bustled away, and I wondered who was she going to send, and how, and why Audrey, of all people. But soon enough she was back, and it couldn't have been more than minutes after she returned when someone knocked at the door.

"Go on," Belinda said, so I went to open it.

Not only Audrey, but Rob and Amy and Dan and Max, too, stood there. They were all wearing smiles, each carrying something, parcels and dishes, and, in Max's case, that silly plaster pig under his arm.

I could not help but be taken aback. "Is this to be a party, then?"

"Why not?" Audrey replied.

"Humor us," said Dan.

"We're just glad you're well," said Amy. "That relapse of yours worried me a bit, I have to admit."

"But the specialist–"

"Even specialists can be wrong," Amy replied. "Especially – well, even in my time, even in Dan's, they're not always right. I can see, simply looking at you, that they were in your case. The exam confirmed it."

"But the tumor–"

She grinned, although something in her eyes looked rather embarrassed. "Good mountain air, good food, good friends, being useful."

"May we come in?" asked Rob.

"Oh! I'm sorry!" I backed up and gestured them all in. "Of course you may."

The little crowd filled our parlor, with barely enough seats for all. I do believe they would have kept on going into the kitchen if Belinda had not stood in the doorway, her hands cradling the big brown teapot.

"I'll fetch the cups and plates, then," Audrey said, and did so before I could do it myself.

Neither she nor Belinda would let me help, either with the tea or with the cakes. But when we were all settled around the little table, they raised their cups, so I did as well. Dan, his eyes twinkling as he gave Rob a sly look, said, "To Conconully."

"To Conconully," they all repeated, so I did, too, and took a sip. The tea was strong and sweet.

I was about to take another, longer drink, when Amy raised her cup, and so did the rest of them. I glanced quizzically at Belinda, but she simply nodded at me, and so I raised mine, too. "To home," Amy said. Oh, yes, I thought. This is home. I still did not understand enough about Conconully, things I needed to put right, doubts I still had, but the one thing I no longer doubted was that I belonged here.

"To home," I repeated with them, and drank. I could feel the hot tea coursing through my body, lighting me up like a lamp.

It was then I realized they were all watching me, as if expecting something from me. And I suddenly knew what it was. I raised my cup. Out of the corner of my eye, I saw Dan smirk at Amy, and her free hand grasp his. I wrapped my own fingers around Belinda's, and smiled at her as I said, "To my new friends."

We drank one more time, and then Audrey refilled cups and passed around cakes. Spice cake. My favorite. But the frosting was new to me, a rich, almost fudgy consistency, tasting like brown sugar and butter.

"Penuche," Audrey told me when I asked her.

"It's delicious. Then again, everything you cook is."

I could feel Belinda's amused gaze on me. "I didn't think you liked spice."

I laughed, but Amy said, "I don't think anyone likes spice in industrial quantities, Belinda. Anyone but you, that is."

"I suppose not." But Belinda was laughing with me, so apparently I had not offended her. Or Amy had not, at any rate.

We had all enjoyed our tea and cake, and Audrey had begun to gather plates and cups, when I thought, I have to know. I closed my eyes briefly, and asked, "Is there nothing to be done about the boy Brian?"

Silence fell abruptly. It went on so long I almost regretted my words. But then I thought about him, living all alone on the fringes of nowhere. He was part of the town, with his parents and the other children, part of the place where he belonged. The community had taken me in, had taken in Amy and Dan, three total strangers, and had made us their own. Brian Whittaker had a family, had lived here all of his life, and yet they ignored his very existence. Couldn't even see him, if Max was to be believed. Had not known he was still alive.

"The poor child is starving, and lonely, and out in the cold. He's made the best of it, for heaven only knows how long, and his family misses him still."

"They do," said Max. "It's even worse now that you've raised their hopes again."

"But he's alive," I said desperately. "He deserves to be able to come home."

The silence this time was profound. Amy was the one who broke it. "He does. The whole point of bringing us here was to change things, to make time start again. What happened to poor Alan Arngrim was part of it. The fact that Oscar Miller was able to bring Claudia here is part of it. Why can't rescuing Brian Whittaker be part of it?"

Her words made little sense to me. Make time start again? Time could not stop. It was the one constant in the world. Yesterday, today, tomorrow. Last year, next year. But then there was my school's record book, no dates, no changes...

"And you all thought *I* was loco because I told you Brian was alive?" I demanded. "What do you mean, make time start again?"

"It already has," Max said firmly. "Yes, we must rescue young Brian. And, if we can, Oscar Miller."

"Oscar, yes. For Rose's sake, if nothing else," Amy added. "Ever since she found out Oscar's still alive she's gotten worse. She's fading. And she deserves to see him before she's gone."

"Fading," I repeated. "Yes. Before young Brian fades away altogether."

They all stared at me. "Do you think that's what's happening?" Amy asked at last.

"The poor boy is starving to death," I told her flatly. "I've been giving him as much food as he'll take, and he wolfs it down, but every time I see him he's thinner, and more ragged, and he's going to die if someone doesn't help him."

I should have said so much sooner. Amy was not the only person in the room who was appalled by my statement. I was beginning to think they actually believed me now. The normally equable Audrey looked as if she was about to burst into tears. "That poor child!" she said at last.

"We must do something," Rob added. He put an arm around his wife.

Belinda had not let go of my hand. She squeezed it. "Whatever I can do, I will."

"Child neglect," said Dan. "That's illegal, at least in my time, and, as sheriff, I say it is here and now, too. We need to take care of him."

"It's immoral in any time," said Max. "Can you bring the boy to us?" This was addressed to me, apparently.

"What good would it do, if you cannot see him?" I asked.

"His sister said she could see him." Max patted the pig, which sat on the floor beside him. "If you can see him, and little Laura can see him, we can work from there."

Dan gave him a dubious look. "You think Harry can fix this? Do you think it *can*?"

I could not help myself. "How can that plaster pig fix anything?"

Max chuckled, but there was a sound in it I did not like. "Do you have any better suggestions? Claudia, you go find the boy. Daniel, you fetch Laura Whittaker. If you can do so without telling her parents for now, I think that would be best."

Amy said, "Bring both children to my office. Yes, Max," as the little man began to protest. "Brian will need my care, and I can do my best for him there."

"I will gather some new clothing for him," Belinda said, and headed for her workroom.

"And I'll fetch him a meal," Audrey added, rising. She took a deep breath and let it out on the word, "Starving!" It was as if she was personally affronted, above and beyond the awfulness of it.

As Amy, Dan, Audrey, and I left, Max and Rob were putting their heads together. I had no idea what they were plotting, but, I thought, fiercely glad, at least they believed me now. We were all on Brian's side.

* * *

Once we were outdoors, Amy pulled me aside. "Can you find him on your own or do you need our help?"

I shrugged. "I don't see what you could do, considering the circumstances."

"I've thought I felt something, on occasion," Dan said. "Like someone was watching me. Trying to get my attention."

Amy whirled on him. "Why didn't you say something before?"

He stared her right back down. "You of all people ought to know why. The first time it happened was the day of the wolf, and I wasn't about to make people think I was crazy. Crazier."

My breath caught. "Wolf? Where, Dan?"

He turned to answer me. "Up at the schoolhouse. The critter's long dead, so you don't have to worry about it."

"It had to be him," Amy said, rather ungrammatically. "Let's go."

"No. You'll frighten him. I'll fetch him." I hoped.

I noticed that the season was beginning to change from spring to summer as I trod determinedly up the hill to the schoolhouse. The leafed-out maples cast a welcome shade against the bright sun, and the grass on the side of the path was knee-deep. I had no idea what I was going to do, how I would find Brian, if he was not there on a Saturday. But where else did he have to go?

I don't think I have ever heard such silence as the kind surrounding my little schoolhouse that afternoon. It was so quiet that the maple leaves seemed to be whispering, their language softer than understanding. It was so still that my feet on the schoolhouse stoop echoed from the boards to the sky and back. I pushed the door open and stepped inside.

"Brian? Are you here? It's Miss Ogden."

I didn't want to tell him I wanted to take him to Doctor Amy's office. I was so frightened of spooking him. When had it become so important that he believe me? When had I begun to believe Max Pepper when he said, "we can work from there." Work from where?

"Brian?" But the boy was not there. Or was he? I could have vowed I heard breathing, shallow and rasping. I followed the source of the sound, to one of the windows I knew I had closed the afternoon before. It stood open now, and I leaned out.

"Teacher?" The raspy voice was faint to the point of non-existence. I looked down. "Oh, Brian!"

"Yes, ma'am." His lips barely moved.

By the time I dashed back out the schoolhouse door and around the corner of the building to him, his eyes were closed. He had obviously fallen – from the roof? a tree? Somewhere far too high. He lay flat on his back, all four limbs splayed wide, his head twisted to one side.

But that was the least of it. He had been thin and ragged before. Now he was almost skeletal, and his clothes fell like rags from his body. His blond hair was dull and thin, his skin so pale – in the few seconds it took me to gather him up in my arms, I thought I could see *through* him to the thick green grass. Even as I did, I could see no impression remaining from his body on the vegetation.

He weighed nothing. I do not mean that figuratively. I mean that I, who had lost so much strength to my illness, could lift him almost effortlessly. As I came around the schoolhouse, I saw Dan striding up the hill toward me.

"My God," he said, coming to a dead stop when he reached us. "*That's* Brian?" but then he shook himself and added, "Let me take him."

"Can you see him?" I asked in shock.

"Never mind. I can see enough."

"I am so afraid," I told him as we eased Brian from my grasp to his. "I think it may be too late."

"Let's hope not." He headed back down the hill. "Max is going to have to work a miracle on this one."

CHAPTER 17

Brian did not wake when Dan took him from my arms. I held the boy's hand in mine as we walked down the hill, absurdly afraid he would vanish altogether if I did not continue to touch him. He did not wake again, either, not when we arrived at Doctor Amy's office, not when Dan placed him carefully on the bed in her examining room.

"Where is Laura?" I asked.

"In the parlor with Belinda and Audrey," Amy replied, already abstracted as she began her examination. "We don't want her terrified."

I could understand that. "But I thought we needed her–"

"Max?" Amy's query was more of a demand, cutting across my voice.

"Yes."

"What do we do now?" She didn't know? I wondered madly. She was supposed to know.

"He's-he's worse than I thought he would be." The little man sounded frightened.

He had no right to be frightened, I thought angrily. "Which means we need to move more quickly. Where is the food? Where is some water? Where is that magical pig you all put so much faith in?"

"Claudia." Amy's voice held a tone in it I did not want to hear. Sadness. No, grief.

"Do not tell me you cannot do anything for him." If they were going to let that child die then they shouldn't have listened to me to begin with.

I let go of Brian for the first time, ignoring the gasps behind me as I strode out to the parlor and went to young Laura Whittaker. I knelt before where she sat on the davenport with Belinda, a picture book in her little hands. "Laura, I'm Miss Ogden. I'm the new schoolteacher."

She gave me an impish grin, a light in what was becoming a bleak place indeed. "Brian likes you."

It had to work. "Brian needs you right now. Could you come with me?"

"Give me the book, Laura," Belinda told her, and took it when the child handed it to her. "Are you sure?" This was directed at me.

"Yes. Everyone else seems to think it's too late, but I am not giving up on that child." It came out a bit more belligerantly than I had intended, but I was extremely tired of not being listened to.

From the door, Amy said, "Come quickly." Then she looked down at Laura, whose hand was clasped firmly in mine. "No, Claudia–"

"Yes." I pushed through. "Max." Formality was beside the point right then, and I was not asking. "Fetch the pig."

He looked helplessly at Amy, who shrugged.

"Where is the sheriff?"

"Right here." And he, bless him, had the pig in his arms.

"Come on." We gathered round the bed, all of us, Belinda and Audrey and Rob, too, and looked down on poor young Brian, but before I could tell Dan to put the pig beside him, and tell everyone – no, I do not know why it needed to be so, but it did – to touch the child somewhere, anywhere, and before I could pick Laura up so she could see him and touch him, too, the raspy, shallow breathing – stopped.

* * *

I did not realize I had been holding my own breath until Laura started squirming in my arms. Before I could stop her she'd half fallen onto the bed to wrap her little arms around the still form of her brother.

It was terrible. It was macabre. But when I reached down to pick her up she would not let go. And it wasn't until Amy breathed, "wait," that I stopped trying. She laid a small, strong hand on Brian's head. Almost as if compelled, Dan rested his larger, calloused hand on the boy's shoulder. Then Audrey, on his arm. Then Rob. Then Belinda. Then Max, his right hand holding Brian's, and, slowly, his left hand settling on that plaster pig. At that very instant, the entire room went still. I stared around at the faces, motionless as that plaster pig, caught in the act of gazing down at Brian.

All immobile except for Max, who looked up at me with, was that hope in his eyes? "It's all right Claudia," he told me. "Do it."

What else could I do? I reached down to rest a hand next to Amy's on Brian's head. My palm on his forehead, my fingers in his lank, stringy hair. But as I did, I heard an inhalation.

"Look," I heard Max murmur, but I was not paying any attention to him whatsoever.

"He's breathing," I whispered. "He's not dead."

"I am," Max said a moment later, "afraid to let go."

"We cannot stand here forever." Indeed, I was feeling a bit lightheaded. I wasn't sure if it was my illness returning, or what was happening in this room, or something else altogether, but, "I need to–"

The room faded, and I felt myself fainting, for the second time in my life. When I came to, I was lying on the bed next to young Brian, who, I was extremely relieved to discover, was still breathing.

"Welcome back," Amy told me.

"I am sorry. Here, let me get out of the way. How is Brian?"

But the little doctor would not let me rise. "He's going to be all right." Then, as I turned to stare at him, "No, I don't know why, or how, but if there's one thing I've learned since I arrived here is it's better not to question Max on some things, especially when he works a miracle like this one. Let me check you over before I let you up." She chuckled at what must have been an expression of consternation on my face. "I'm sure it was only a faint, but humor me. It'll only take a minute."

She was true to her word, but then she called Belinda in to help her get me on my feet, and said, rather to my dismay, "Take her home and put her to bed, will you?"

"I'm fine," I protested.

"Humor me," Amy said again, but Belinda shook her head.

"We'll sit down in the parlor for a bit, Amy."

Amy looked as if she was considering continuing the argument, but a faint young voice from the bed said, "Teacher?" and that settled the matter.

Rob and Audrey went to fetch the children's parents, who had just begun to miss Laura and to search for her, I understood, but who forgave all and sundry, including those who did not need forgiving, when they discovered their son alive and well in Doctor Amy's examining room bed. I sat by the bed in a chair the sheriff brought for me, and kept a hand in Brian's, still ridiculously reluctant to let go of him.

The reunion was all I could have hoped for, and soothed my own raw feelings on the subject of Brian's abandonment. It wasn't, I finally understood, a willful rejection of the boy; they truly had thought he was dead. I watched Brian's joyful face peeping over his mother's shoulder, his father's arms around them both, and eventually I felt able, albeit slowly and carefully, to slip my hand from his.

He did not, much to my relief, faint or begin to fade again. I glanced up at Belinda, looking for reassurance, but her expression reflected those of the reunited family. She smiled down at me. "Thank you."

I ducked my head. "I'm still not sure what it was I did." Slowly, I stood, Belinda's strong hand under my elbow, although at the moment I did not feel the need for her support. I did not shrug her off, however. Her hand felt good there. Right.

I glanced out the window and gasped. I do believe the entire town was out there, smiling and waving.

"Word gets out fast," said Dan, coming up to my other side.

I turned to him. "I don't suppose you had anything to do with that?"

He shrugged, obviously unrepentant. "I might have. Don't worry. I can handle the crowd control." Before I could comment on that odd statement, he paused, then said slowly, "I wonder if you'd be willing to try another experiment."

"Was that what this was? I thought we were rescuing a child."

He said hastily, "You were. You did. It was fantastic."

And what was I supposed to say to that? Fantastical was certainly the right word "Did you know—"

But Max was bustling up. "You'd better get out there, Daniel, before someone gets trampled in the excitement."

"Yeah, yeah." And he strode off, to do heaven only knew what with the throng. I could almost feel the air vibrate from the voices and movement outside and it was a marvelous feeling to know everyone out there was as happy as those of us in that room. I glanced over to where

Brian and his family were still radiating joy like the sun on a summer day, and basked in it. I had never been a part of anything like this before, and at that moment I did not care if I would ever understand what had happened, or how it had come to take place.

If I did nothing else in this life, I had helped that boy survive, and brought him home where he would be loved and cared for again. Where he belonged. It was more than enough.

Eventually Belinda, with Amy's help, persuaded me to go back home. We slipped out the back door and across Amy's little wild garden, down the empty back streets past the tidy homes and under the arching maples, now in full leaf. I stopped, staring. "It doesn't look like it did when I first arrived."

"Well, it's been weeks," Belinda said practically. "Summer's all but arrived."

"No. When I first came here, it looked different." I tried to remember what I had seen when I first came over the rise and saw the town spread out below me. The memory was disturbingly vague.

I felt Belinda's hand under my elbow again, nudging me along. "I know you have to be tired, dear. Let's go along home."

"Home. Yes." I shook my head and started forward again. Did it matter what I'd thought I'd seen what was beginning to feel like a very long time ago? No, it couldn't. I knew what I was seeing now, and I liked it very much. If part of me still didn't understand the miracles I'd seen since I'd arrived here – not only Brian's rescue, but my own health – did I really want to know how they'd happened?

I don't know whether I am ashamed or not to say that, yes, I did.

We climbed the steps to the back door of our house. I fancied it felt welcoming, as if I was a part of its existence that had been missing before, and was complete now. Perhaps I was. I turned to take Belinda's hands, then to hug her. She smiled at me, and hugged me back, but then she said firmly, "You need to rest," took me to my room, and helped me into bed.

Her backward glance was fond, but disconcertingly a bit worried, as she closed the door behind her. After I listened to her steps down the stairs, I stood up and went to the mirror. I did not know what it was she saw that made her so concerned about me, but I thought I had never looked healthier in my life, rumpled dress, tumbled hair, and all.

CHAPTER 18

The celebration of young Brian's return, as people insisted on calling the event in spite of the fact that he'd never left, would be fairly subdued, according to Max, who came to see me the next day after church. Whether this was in his capacity as minister, or mischief-maker in chief, I wasn't sure, but I was on my guard, anyway.

"Due to his age, and his illness, we're not going to throw a party."

I did believe Max when he said Brian was going to be all right, eventually, but the boy had some way to go. "I hadn't expected you would."

"We haven't thrown one for you yet, either." His eyes twinkled at me.

This took me aback. "I should certainly hope not!"

"We would, you know. That tea party wasn't much."

"That tea party was more than enough." I paused. "You would do it even against my will?"

"You'll have to ask Sheriff Reilly about that one. Or perhaps our Doctor Duvall." Max looked like he was settling in for a long conversation, and I was very grateful when a knock sounded at the door.

I had no sooner gotten up to answer it when the knob turned, the door opened, and Timothy Fogle, one of my younger pupils, stuck his head inside. "Miss Ogden?"

"Yes, Tim?" I could hear the relief in my voice, even if I could feel Max's self-satisfied expression aimed at my back.

"You're wanted at the Sheriff's." Before I could ask why, he ducked back out and the door closed with rather more force than he must have intended, because an "I'm sorry, Miss Ogden," floated back through the open window over the sound of his trotting footsteps.

I turned back to Max, but he was already rising and heading for the door.

What did Sheriff Reilly want with me? The only thing I could think of was that one of my students had gotten into trouble, but if that was the case, his parents would be the ones called for.

Apparently Max was as curious as I, because whether I liked it or not, he accompanied me on the short walk to the main street and on to the small white clapboard house, shaded by a maple enormous even for its kind. It served the sheriff as both office and home, at least until he and the young doctor were married.

But when I climbed the steps, Mr. Pepper hung back. "Come along," I said impatiently. "You know you will, anyway."

He merely grinned and nodded, and stood beside me as I knocked on the door.

It opened almost immediately. To my surprise, Belinda stood there. I had thought she'd gone back to work in her shop after all of the hullabaloo, and what was she doing here? She gestured us in as if it were her own home.

The sheriff's parlor cum office was crowded with the inner circle, as I was beginning to think of them. Rob, Dan, Amy, Belinda, and, as

Max seated himself on one of three empty chairs remaining, Audrey bustled in with a tray. Of course. I hastily sat down as well.

Belinda, sitting next to me, gave my hand a squeeze. I glanced over at her.

"So," Dan said, without any preamble, as Audrey poured tea and passed slices of cake, "We know it can be done."

"Do you know if it should be done again?" Max demanded.

It was as if I had walked into the middle of an ongoing discussion, one Max jumped right into as if he'd already been here when I arrived.

"If what should be done?" I asked, although I thought I knew what they were talking about.

"He deserves to see her," Audrey stated as if to brook no argument.

Rob argued, anyway. "To lose her again?"

Belinda said, the quality of her voice utterly unlike her normal calm confidence, "perhaps it would stop—"

"We don't have the right to play God." Max's flat voice brought the argument to a dead stop.

After a moment, I opened my mouth, but before I could speak, Amy said, in a tone I couldn't quite decipher, "I thought that was your *job*, Max."

Well. And so. That explained more than I had ever wanted to know. He'd told me his story, about the salted mine, and the pig, and his get rich scheme gone horribly wrong, but he had cast himself as another victim in the telling.

Which he was, I supposed. It wasn't as if he'd known the flood was going to happen, or that Harry the pig was some sort of magical – whatever it was. Or had he?

"Mr. Pepper—" I began, but he interrupted me.

"Max. Please call me Max."

I shook my head impatiently. "You're not from Conconully, are you?"

He stared at me. "I've been living here for–" And it was his turn to look bewildered, the expression on his face acquiring that now-familiar vague cast to it, his eyes looking rather lost. I had seen it often enough on others' faces when I had asked for answers to questions they'd long since given up consideration to.

But it was the first time I'd seen such an expression on Max's face. And, as I looked around the circle, the, was that fear? on their faces told me his confusion was something they'd never seen before, either.

Then Max shook his head, and smiled, but his sudden cheerfulness did not go all the way to his eyes. "This is the result we aimed to achieve, remember? Why we brought the two of you here," he gestured at Dan and Amy, "and why we were so glad when you arrived, Claudia." He paused. "Alan Arngrim's death was a sad occasion, although I suspect he would have wished us to be happy for him. He's with his dear wife now, which is no more than he ever wanted."

I heard a mutter of, "if you believe in such things," and glanced over at Dan. Amy patted his arm, the gesture as audible to me as a "hush" would have been from anyone else. Belinda's hand tensed as well and I shook my head slightly.

"What does this have to do with Oscar and Rose?" Dan demanded. "For all you know, he's as stuck as you folks were before you started monkeying with the machinery."

"Not just for all we know," said Belinda. "Tell him, Claudia." She squeezed my hand again, I supposed in encouragement, but I was baffled.

"What year was it when you left Seattle?"

I blinked. "1910." I nodded at Dan and Amy. "I told you that before."

No one gasped. No one's eyes widened. They took this peculiar anomaly in stride as Belinda said, "Not 1893. But we knew that. How old did Mr. Miller look to you?"

I thought back. It wasn't easy. I knew how I'd arrived here. I knew who I was, what I had been, what I was now. I still knew I hadn't always lived in Conconully, although it felt like it, and I knew now I always wanted to live here. But my former life, in all its details, had fallen farther away in my memory. I knew this forgetfulness was not the normal way of things, the way one's childhood becomes rosier the older one becomes. I knew part of it was this place, and the, I could not think of another word, the magic here. I did not regret it, because I was well and whole and happy, for the first time in my life. And if I never grew old, never –

"He told me. He was sixty-three."

Now they did gasp. At least some of them did. Audrey said, "That can't be right. Are you sure?"

"Yes. Why?"

"Because," Rob declared, "the last time I saw him, the day before the flood, was his birthday. He was sixty-three years old then. Max." He turned to fix his gaze on the little man, who was, to my astonishment, scooting back in his chair. "We must do something."

"He's as stuck in limbo as we are," Amy sounded almost as if she was pleading. "And Rose with him. She should have faded long ago. What if she can't? Until she sees him again?"

I have never seen a man look quite so stunned. It took him longer to recover this time, too. At last he shook his head. "I wish I had never gone down that mine," he said at last. "I have caused more pain, more suffering, than I could have wished on my worst enemies, and instead I did it to the people who have become my best friends. All I wanted to do was make things better."

"And get rich in the process." But Dan sounded more amused than anything else. "Don't we all."

Max stared off into the distance for a moment, as if seeing something the rest of us could only guess at. At last he said, "We have three days till Oscar makes his next delivery."

Nods went around the circle, including, to my amusement, my own. I had no idea how he knew this, but if I had learned one thing about my new home, it was not to question the accepted wisdom. Most of which seemed to emanate from a man who had apparently set something in motion and was struggling madly to figure out how to stop it.

"More tea?" Audrey asked the group. "We might as well decide how we're going to do this now."

It was late afternoon by the time Belinda and I made our way back home. "I have lesson plans to put together," I told her as we climbed the steps.

She nodded, as if still a bit dazed. I couldn't blame her. Apparently, until I came along she'd had no idea what held this town together. So far as I could tell, that knowledge had been held tightly among Max, Audrey, and Rob, until Daniel, Amy, and I had arrived. Belinda was only part of it now because of me. But the rest of the townspeople seemed to have no idea why they never aged, why they never had contact with the outside world.

"Except for us."

"I beg your pardon?"

I turned from where I had opened the door to my little study. "Did I say that out loud?"

"You said, except for us. What did you mean?"

"What was it like for you before you knew what is really happening here?"

She paused, then said, "I don't know."

"You don't know, or you don't remember?"

Instead of answering me, she asked, "Do you regret having come here?"

I shook my head. "I can't. If I hadn't come here, I would not be well, and, as important, I would not have met you."

"Would you go back?" She cocked her head at me, in a way that was achingly familiar now. "If you knew you could keep your health? Would you want to go back to Seattle?"

"No," I said firmly. "I belong here. With you." I thought of Jean, and the decisions she'd made, and how grateful I was to her. "I do wish– well, but that's water over the dam. Jean wasn't happy here. She is happy where she is. I doubt she misses me any more than I've missed her."

"But you feel as if you ought to."

I shrugged. "She saved my life, every bit as much as this place did, or Doc Amy. Or Oscar Miller, which is why we have to try to help him and Rose. Or you. You're the one who really saved my life, Belinda. Don't you know that?"

She came to me, put her arms around me. "No, dearest. You saved mine."

The plans went forward. No one seemed to question why the six of us spent so much time together, or why I cut classes short Monday and Tuesday afternoon. None of us questioned Max's knowledge of when Oscar was to arrive, either. And when I went to the Whittakers' house on Wednesday afternoon to ask if I might take Brian and Laura for a walk, not a question was asked.

Laura bounced like an India rubber ball, her small hand where she hung onto mine warm and real. But Brian, in spite of the rapid improvement in his health, seemed hesitant, and the trust I'd lost from him hurt my heart. He wanted to know where we were going, which, of course, I could not say truthfully in front of his parents, but I knew he did not believe me.

And when we met with the others at the edge of town, he hung back. "Teacher?"

"It's all right, Brian."

"Hey, Brian," Dan said. He was the only one of us carrying anything, Harry the pig tucked under his arm like a small barrel. His other hand had a firm grip on Amy's, not that she seemed to be complaining. Rob clasped Audrey's as well, and I wished I could have been holding Belinda's, but my hands were full with the children, and Belinda, although she still seemed uneasy with the entire situation, smiled at me when I glanced over at her.

Max was the only one who seemed apart from us all.

It was a relief to me when Laura yanked her hand from mine and ran to Rob, who scooped her up in his free arm, where she sat looking like a small princess in her pink dress and matching hair ribbon.

Brian did not seem encouraged by this, but did not let go of me, either. And when Belinda reached out for the hand Laura had relinquished, I gripped it firmly and felt reassured.

Max snorted. "So we're all sorted out now?" he said, and was that a trace of bitterness in his voice?

"Almost," Rob said. "We still need to fetch Rose."

I could see Max's chest rise with his breath, ready to let loose the argument once more. It was the only thing we had disagreed on, all of us against him.

"Max," Audrey said, in that firm tone even he had been forced to listen to, "it's her right. We're doing this for her."

168

"And if it doesn't work?" He sounded almost desperate. "What will we tell her then?"

But Amy was already knocking on the door of the little cottage where Rose lived.

"It's too late now," Dan told Max, who was now jittering as if someone had pulsed an electric current through him.

Amy knocked again. "Rose? Please come to the door." She turned the knob and opened it. "Oh, dear God."

We were too late.

CHAPTER 19

She was so still, so quiet. So almost transparent. She looked as Brian had before we'd brought Laura to him, before she and that pig, and our touch, had brought him back to us. Laura squirmed down from where Rob held her, and ran to the – husk? – lying crumpled on the wooden floor.

"Gramma Rose?" Rose was not the child's grandmother, wasn't anyone's grandmother since, as Belinda had told me, she'd never had children. All of the children gave her the courtesy title, however, and I had never thought to wonder why. It was, I realized suddenly, because it wasn't a courtesy. As Laura knelt before her, patting her face, I knew that was how she thought of Rose.

Brian was still hanging back. I think if I had not been holding onto him, he would have run away altogether. But Laura jumped up, grabbed his free hand, and with a strength beyond her size and years, pulled her reluctant brother down next to Rose's – no, Rose, not Rose's body. As the children touched her, I saw her chest rise with a shallow breath.

In the next instant, Daniel dropped down on her other side, setting the pig next to her. And Audrey, and Rob, and Max, and Belinda.

And me.

I realized I was holding my own breath, and let it out in a whoosh.

Nothing was happening. No, that was not true. She had not been breathing before Laura touched her. She was breathing now. But she was not waking up, not as Brian had. She was no less transparent than she had been, but she was not becoming more – real? opaque? than she had been, either. She was hanging, I suddenly realized, between life and wherever she was headed – heaven? But she could not go, and could not stay.

When Max reached out for that pig, I said, not knowing why but knowing I must, "No, Max. Don't touch it. We need to find Oscar and we need to do it now. Before she goes."

I had never seen an apparatus like the one now before me in my life. Rob dashed off down through town and, moments later, came back driving a, a, I suppose one would call it a horseless carriage, for lack of a better term. The machines had become popular in Seattle in the last few years, although still rare enough that carriage drivers complained of how they spooked the horses, and pedestrians gave the noisy, clanking monsters an extremely wide berth.

This one did not look or sound like one of those. In appearance it was more like an abbreviated streetcar than anything else, but it was not connected to any overhead wires or strips of metal teeth in the street. Indeed, how could it have been when there were no such devices in Conconully? The vehicle was bright red where its paint was not nicked and scarred, the cab, as I later learned it was called, completely enclosed with glass windows, one of which disappeared as I watched, apparently sliding down into a slot in the metal door of the contraption. It rumbled and purred like a large cat, rather than rattle and snort and shake like a normal horseless carriage. It had one long padded seat inside, patched and repatched with silvery tape. And the entire back of the beast was open to the sky like a horsedrawn wagon.

"Here, wait a minute, let me get the tailgate," Dan said, and lowered the back side of the open space. Belinda, Amy, and Audrey had already gone back inside the house. I shook myself and drew my gaping gaze away to go help, as Dan lifted Laura into the back of the – bed? It was obviously for the same use as the bed of a wagon. Brian, his misgivings apparently erased by the excitement and novelty of the adventure, scrambled up after her.

"You two hang on," Dan told him. "Claudia, you get on up there and hold onto both of them. And he lifted me up into the open back with all the manners of a gentleman helping me into a carriage, if such a carriage had been three feet off the ground with no steps.

Awkwardly I settled myself into a corner under the back window of the enclosure. Laura immediately came and snuggled up next to me, and I pulled Brian down by the hand until he sat, fidgeting, on my other side. It was not the most comfortable of seating arrangements. The floor of the bed was corrugated in a manner guaranteed to prevent it.

Then a blanket flew over the side, and a second one. I began to spread them out, assuming Rose would be lying on them, when Amy came to the still lowered end of the vehicle. "Those are for us. You three sit on one along one side, and spread the other one on the other side of the truck bed for us. We've got more blankets for Rose."

I started to get back to my feet. "Wait a moment. I will come back and help."

"No. Stay there. We've got this."

Brian helped me fold and arrange the blankets for padding, and we settled back down in a bit more comfort, as Dan boosted Amy into the bed, then climbed up after her. They both turned to lift one end of a pallet. Rose lay upon it, thin and frail and even more transparent in the bright sunlight. Careful not to jolt her, they, and Audrey, Max, and Rob on the other end, nudged the pallet into the space, then Rob picked up a sputtering Max and plunked him in with us, and lifted the panel to close the box, latching it with a metallic clang.

"What *is* this contraption?" I finally managed to ask as our fellow passengers settled themselves on the blanket opposite, Dan, with Harry the pig next to him, then Amy, then Max. I could feel the weight of the truck move under us as Audrey, Belinda, and Rob climbed into the front enclosure.

"It's a truck," Dan said. "Long story. Hold on."

"Oh, good grief," Amy said, peering through the window. "Audrey's driving. What on earth possessed Rob to let her have the wheel? Hang on."

To what? I thought, and put one arm around each of the children.

The jolt as the truck moved forward did not quite throw me out of the back, but it wasn't for lack of trying on its part. We bounced over rut and bump with a carelessness that made me hang onto the children with all of my strength as we moved forward, up the hill and around the bend out of town, faster than I would have ever thought possible.

The wind blew my hat off of my head before I could catch it, and I watched it bounce down the road behind us with some regret. It had been my favorite. I supposed I could have asked to stop and retrieve it, but it seemed petty at that moment.

Once we reached the forest, and the road turned into nothing more than a track, ironically, we were not jounced around so much. I could hear the green grass of early summer whipping against the metal sides of the vehicle, and could not help but be reminded of my ride in Mr. Miller's wagon on the way here. Would I see that wagon again? I knew I would not be tempted to return with him, even if he and Rose left us to return to the outside world. This was my place, and I was grateful to him for being part of the destiny, as I could not help but think of it now, that had brought me here.

A tug on my hand brought me back. Little Laura was grinning up at me as if she were on a carnival ride, and the excitement of both children was palpable. I glanced up to see Max, whose expression changed quickly from one I could not decipher to a firm nod of satisfaction.

"Quite a ride!" he shouted. I nodded, not willing to bellow back at him.

I hoped we did not have much farther to go, and, as it turned out, we didn't, although the ride seemed much longer than it actually was. My body still felt as if the truck was moving and I in it, even after Dan helped me down over the lowered tailgate.

The woods seemed so much more quiet, and, as I gazed around me, somehow familiar.

"The barrels aren't here yet," Audrey said. "We're not too late."

Even as she spoke, I thought I heard the creak of wagon wheels and the soft jingle of harness. I wasn't the only one to hear it, either. We all, except for Rose, and Amy who had stayed with her after the men had lifted her pallet down from the bed of the truck, stood in a group near the back of the open tailgate. But as the sounds grew louder, even the children fell silent.

If I had closed my eyes, I would have vowed anything that I could see that wagon. The sounds became louder and louder, until a man's voice, Mr. Miller's voice, said, "Whoa, there, boys," and the sounds of a moving wagon came to an abrupt halt.

But I could not see him. Not with my eyes wide open. I felt Laura and Brian go very still, and I glanced down to see them not frightened, exactly, but wary. I could not blame them. Wary did not begin to describe how I felt.

"Oscar?" Max sounded far more tentative and uncertain than I had ever heard him. "Rose is here. She needs you."

"Max Pepper. You son of a bitch." The curse was not friendly. Mr. Miller was angry; no, he was absolutely livid. So much so that I could not help but gather the children closer to me, even though I knew neither they nor I was the focus of that concentrated rage. Something – some *one* – thumped down from the truck: a shadow, as if shadows had weight and heft and fury. "You told me Rose was dead. I knew she wasn't, but you wouldn't help her. You wouldn't help me."

I will have to give credit to the little man. He stood his ground. "I was wrong, Oscar. I know I was wrong. I couldn't help you then, and I don't know if I can help you now. But Rose is here, and so are you, and so am I." He held his hands out to the empty air. "But she's fading. If I could change the past, I would, but I can't. If I could change anything, I would never have set foot in that mine. I would never have – no, I would not have condemned us all to die in that flood. I couldn't."

"You did what you could," said Rob.

How did I know the shadow whirled on him? "Easy for you to say. You haven't been separated from your life for eternity."

Rob said no more, but he bowed his head and his arm went around Audrey as if he thought she would be torn away from him then and there.

"Rose is here now, Oscar," Max said, sounding more than a bit desperate.

"And I can't see her. Can't touch her. Haven't you tortured me enough?"

Max's chest rose visibly with the breath he drew in. "I think I know how you can now. Come here. Take my hand." After a moment, and the sound of another drawn-in breath that seemed to come from nowhere, I could see Max's stubby fingers wrap around something I still couldn't see. He pulled on it, and led the way to where Rose was lying on her pallet on the soft grass.

"Dan, would you please bring Harry to us?"

Silently, Dan lifted the pig from the bed of the truck and set it next to where Max, and presumably Mr. Miller, were kneeling beside Rose.

"Everyone, come round and join hands." We did so, completely surrounding the pallet except for where Max was, and the shadowed space next to him. "Claudia, can you see Oscar?"

"No." But that wasn't completely honest. "I can tell where he is. There's a shadow—"

"All right." But I could hear the relief in his voice. "You come sit next to him."

Reluctantly, I put Laura's hand in Belinda's, and brought Brian around with me, putting him to my left. On my right was Max, and between us that space, not empty to any sense but the visual.

"Can you touch him?" Max asked.

I swallowed. "I don't know."

"Try."

It took all of my courage to reach out, but when I did, I felt a flannel-covered shoulder as real and firm as my own body. With an unutterable sense of relief, I settled my hand more comfortably and said, trying to keep the quiver out of my voice, "I have him."

The shoulder was still and hard, as if its owner was holding his breath. I gave it a squeeze, and felt it slump, as if I had shared the release of tension with him.

"Teacher?" Brian said, sounding frightened.

"It's all right, Brian."

"Yes, I think it will be," said Rob. "Go on, Max." With his booted foot, he gently nudged the pig closer to Max.

"Yes." With one hand on the shadow that was Mr. Miller, and Rob's big, calloused palm on his shoulder, Max slowly put out his hand and, after hesitating one last second, reached for Harry the pig. As he did, for an instant, I thought I saw Oscar Miller, his weatherbeaten face full of hope, and Rose, solid and opaque and real once more, her eyes open and clear and full of love. Just for an instant, I saw them smile and reach for one another.

Then, as Max's fingers touched Harry's plaster skin, the world went abruptly still and silent and black.

CHAPTER 20

I don't know for how long the world went away, for seconds or an eternity. I do know that when it came back, and thank God it did, I drew in breath as if I hadn't breathed in a lifetime, as if afraid I would never be able to take in air again. I sat in the grass, blinking stupidly, my left hand still clasped firmly in the boy Brian's, and my right –

"He's gone! Oscar's gone." I looked down at the now-empty pallet. "And Rose."

"They both are," said Max. I could see where tears had trickled down his cheeks. As I watched, two more drops slid from his eyes. "They're together, as they should have been all along. As they would have been if I hadn't interfered. As I should have helped them be long ago." He brought his hands to his face, hiding it. His voice was muffled and anguished. "I wish I had never seen that damned pig." He stared around at the faces of our companions. "I am so sorry. I wish I had never thought I was saving this town."

It was Audrey who broke the silence. "No use crying over spilt milk."

"You did save this town," said Belinda. It was the first she'd spoken since we'd left the house. "I remember the flood. We all do."

Dan's face darkened. "I remember the first time I saw you touch that pig. I thought you were all out of your collective tree." Then he smiled, and suddenly I could perceive what it was the young doctor saw in him. "Turns out I was the crazy one. Why do you think I came back?"

"I thought it was for me." But Amy was smiling, too.

"You know, folks," put in Rob. "We've got a party to plan."

I stared at him, at the others as they all nodded, if not with enthusiasm, then with palpable relief. "You're going to celebrate *this*?"

But as we all rose and headed back toward the truck, Audrey gathering the now-empty blankets, Belinda drew me aside. "It's a beautiful day. Let's walk back to town."

By now I was glad to get away from them. From reminders of what I had just seen. "All right." We stepped aside as the truck, loaded with the rest of our company and Rob at the wheel this time, rumbled back off down the hill.

When it was out of sight, Belinda took my hand. Her fingers were warm and familiar, and gave me the reassurance I needed to ask again. "They're not celebrating two deaths with a party, are they?"

"Not deaths," Belinda said as we started up the rise. "Not like poor Mr. Arngrim last New Year's. We don't know where people go when they fade away, but I like to think they're together, either out in the world or in heaven, or perhaps they consider it both. I hope so."

"But to celebrate it–" I couldn't quite bring myself to go on.

"No. The timing is coincidental, or perhaps not, but at least it's not cause and effect. We always have a party on May 26th, to celebrate our resurrection from the flood."

"Oh. What kind of party?" The date had completely escaped me. I hadn't thought people kept track of dates here, so I had quit paying attention myself. "Is it still May?"

She smiled gently up at me. "For a few more days. You'll want a new dress. I happen to have one I finished yesterday that might fit you."

"Do you?" I couldn't help feeling pleased. "I feel terrible not being able to pay you, though."

"You spend your days teaching the children of this town. You've earned it, and everything else you've received since you arrived here. And," she added before I could tell her none of those children were hers, "the children's parents provide for me. It all comes around in the end."

"I suppose." I paused. "All right." And because I couldn't help myself, "What color is it? What design?"

She laughed, and the sound was a balm to me. "You'll see."

By the time we reached town, and our house, I had learned all about the party. About how the young people would decorate the community hall, and how everyone would dress in his or her finest to dance to music provided by Miss Grady the pianist. How she would be accompanied by three brothers who had been playing their instruments since childhood, but who had to be restrained from playing nothing but what the sheriff called "riffs." These were, Belinda explained, long, loud pieces with no melody whatsoever, which no one had ever heard of until Dan had come to town and taught the boys how to play them.

"They're dreadful," Belinda confided to me. "But they make the sheriff happy, and Max says it's good to have new things now and again. Some of the young people actually seem to enjoy the, I hesitate to call them songs. I would appreciate them more if they actually sounded like something besides caterwauling." She hesitated. "I should tell you."

"What is it you need to tell me?" Her tone had changed with that last sentence, from gentle amusement to something approaching worry.

She hesitated, then said, "I need to tell you. Harry, and what happened this afternoon, will be part of this, too."

A chill ran down my spine in spite of the warm sun as we came out of the trees. "What do you mean?"

She didn't answer for a moment.

"Do you mean–" But surely she couldn't mean what had happened when Max put his hand on that plaster pig.

But she nodded. "It's only for a moment, Claudia. And it's necessary."

I knew my eyes were wide. I could feel my breath coming fast and shallow. But then she stopped walking, and me with her, and her arms went around me, and I knew as I felt her affection for me and mine for her that I would do anything, go through anything, to stay here.

She had been quite serious about how important the party was to the town. On Saturday, Belinda's shop was inundated with customers, buying from a stock, she told me, she'd been creating since the last big party, which had taken place on New Year's Eve. And not only clothing, but ribbons and combs and hats and other accoutrements for men and women, adults and children.

I found myself pitching in, helping people find what they were looking for, and taking in a wide variety of goods in barter for the various items. Some were basic and useful like foodstuffs and IOUs for various services we would need over the coming months. Some, I must say, were not. But we accepted everything with great good will, because, as Belinda told me, what we could not use ourselves we could trade for things we did.

By the time the shop closed in the midafternoon, and the last straggler left, I was amazed at what we'd taken in, and what had gone out.

"A good day's work," Belinda told me, nodding firmly.

"Conconully is a larger town than I would have thought," I said in return. "I never suspected so many people lived here, and every one of them must have come into your shop today."

"Oh, you didn't see the half of it. Wait until tonight. Everyone in town will be at the party tonight." She sounded excited, and I must say it was infectious. "You've been very helpful to me, and haven't even asked about your dress."

"I-I didn't have time to get a word in."

"Well, come along. You've earned it." She led me back from the shop into our house, up the stairs to my bedroom, and opened the door with a flourish. "What do you think?"

I could not find my breath. At first all I saw was a vision in the color of pearls. Not gray. Not white. Nothing so shimmeringly glorious could be described using words so drab as those. From a delicately tucked bodice the skirt swept down in graceful folds to the floor, with sleeves that flowed like water and a collar and cuffs in a purely elegant style I had never seen before.

"I wanted fabric to match your eyes, and a simple design. Too many furbelows would compete with your natural looks." Belinda said. "I hope it suits you."

"It's beautiful," I managed at last. This vision matched my eyes? My plain gray eyes? And she thought this was simple? Would suit *me*?

She moved behind me and began undoing the buttons down the back of my shirtwaist. "Let's see what it looks like in its proper place."

Like a doll I stood there and let her undress me, and I imagined her hands touching me along the way, not sure if her motions were real or not. When at last I was arrayed, she stepped back and looked me up and down in obvious satisfaction. "Yes. It suits you. You will shine tonight, as you deserve to."

I looked down. She thought I deserved this. That I would shine. I had never shone like this in my life, and I felt terror and jubilation in equal measure. "It's not–" I took a breath, but could not fill my lungs, and not because of my corset, which Belinda had relaced a fraction tighter than I was used to. I tried again. "It's not too showy for a schoolteacher?"

"It's perfect for you." But she lost her smile, and I regretted my question. Slowly, she said, "People will know, and understand, that it was a gift. And they will know it came from me. They won't say anything, but some may wonder. If that makes you uncomfortable, I understand."

I flung my arms around her, heedless of the dress, and of everything else including my fears. Her arms went around me, too, and I could feel her warmth through the layers of fabric.

"I want to shine," I told her, my voice muffled as I buried my face in her hair. "For you."

After she left, I could not help but admire myself in the glass as I struggled to arrange my hair in a fashion that would do justice to the glorious dress. By the time I came downstairs, Belinda was already there in a gown of deep russet that brought out the silver gleams in her black hair, and made her brown eyes glow. Or perhaps the latter was the fault of how her expression lit up when she saw me, so perhaps the rest of me was not such a disaster in comparison to the dress after all, or at least not in her eyes.

"Shall we be off to Cassandra's?" she asked.

"Flowers?" I felt as if I was drawing enough attention to myself already, but I could not resist.

"We can't arrive in style without them."

And so, after some deliberation among the gorgeous array at the flower shop, Belinda picked a nosegay out for me, consisting of bright blue bachelor's buttons nestled in a spray of delicate little blossoms I'd never seen before but that Cassandra called linaria. I bestowed a bold cluster of early lilies in a glowing gold on Belinda, who, to my surprise and the amusement of the quiet little flower-seller, became as tongue-tied as I when I first saw my dress.

"You said we couldn't arrive without flowers," I told her.

"These– these are too much."

But under her embarrassment I had never seen her looking so pleased. "No more so than my dress." Considerably less, in my opinion.

At last she gave me a helpless smile. "For two spinsters, we make quite the pair."

"The two of you look happy," said Cassandra from behind us. I started and turned, having quite forgotten she was there, but she was watching me with the oddest expression. "Which is as it should be, given what you've done for us."

She could have meant many things, I supposed, but I was fairly sure she'd been hearing my story from someone. Max, perhaps, or more probably Audrey or Dan. I sighed helplessly, but I could not help smiling at her, and, as the door closed behind us, Belinda gave my hand a surreptitious squeeze behind our skirts. Tongue-tied, I let her perform the pleasantries as we passed more of Cassandra's customers on her front porch. Could what I'd started really be this simple, this blameless? I sincerely hoped so.

CHAPTER 21

I find myself at a loss for words to describe the party, bright and gay as it was. Heat and light and color seemed to swirl about me as Belinda and I sat in chairs near one wall and watched the dancers. My feet tapped to the tune of waltzes and reels and schottisches, and, yes, "riffs," where Dan and Amy and a few of the younger people went out on the dance floor and, so far as I could tell, bounced around and shook their entire bodies without any rhythm to it whatsoever. They did look like they were enjoying themselves, though, and, as Belinda whispered in my ear, change was a good thing, even if it seemed a bit odd.

Some time after the music settled back down to something I recognized, a gentleman came up and bowed to both of us. I thought I recognized him from the bustle at the shop this afternoon, but I could not have put a name to his face any more than I could have for the several dozen others who had passed through. But Belinda did, and seemed pleased.

"Claudia, this is Mr. Jasper Kincaid. He runs the mill. Jasper, this is Miss Claudia Ogden, our new schoolteacher."

"Miss Ogden." He took my proffered hand and shook it, rather than raising it to his lips, for which I was grateful. His hand was warm and calloused. He seemed friendly enough, but what was I to say? "Do you like to dance?" he asked me.

I glanced helplessly over at Belinda, but she was smiling in an encouraging manner. Well, and it was not as if we two could dance together, and I supposed I had made it too obvious I would have liked to be out on the floor. I turned slightly away from Mr. Kincaid and mouthed, "I'm sorry."

But Belinda simply shook her head, still smiling at me.

I rose from my seat. "Thank you, Mr. Kincaid, I would like to dance."

The tune was unfamiliar to me, but the rhythm was not. As Mr. Kincaid's arm went round me and I clasped his other hand in mine in the familiar motions of the waltz, I let myself enjoy the movement and rhythm as I had never felt comfortable doing so before. I was not attracted to him, although I suspected I should feel flattered that he, an important man in town, had asked me to dance. He seemed as happy as I was simply to dance, however. When the tune ended and another began, another gentleman introduced himself and I allowed myself to be swept away again, and after that another, and another, until I was breathless and ready to go back to find Belinda and my seat again.

I had felt her watching me, as if she was enjoying herself through me and my innocent pleasure. The words hung unspoken but understood. As long as you come back to me, take your joy where you can. As if I would ever go anywhere, with anyone else but her.

"Thank you," I said to the last gentleman— had I even noted his name? as he walked me back to my seat. Every partner I'd danced with had been a perfect gentleman, and this fellow was no exception. He grinned at Belinda as he helped me to my chair, and I dabbed at the perspiration on my face with my handkerchief. The room was warm, and the air close.

A glass full of amber liquid appeared in front of me, and I took it from Belinda's hand. "You look as if you could use refreshment," she said. "Did you enjoy yourself?"

"Oh, yes," I told her. "I haven't danced like that since I can't remember when."

"I'm glad."

"Do you not dance?" But even as the question hung in the air, I saw a stir at the other end of the room, as Rob boosted Mr. Pepper onto the stage. He looked like a dapper little bird in his top hat and tails. An agitated little bird, as he poked behind the curtain and under the cloth-covered table, then leaned down to say something to Rob and Audrey, who then disappeared behind the curtains.

Belinda rose, and I with her, but she waved me down again. "I'll only be a moment."

I watched her, then the sheriff and the little doctor, make their way down the room to the stage. No one else seemed to be noticing what was going on. The music had stopped, yes, but only, so it seemed, because the musicians needed refreshment as much as the rest of us did. I took a sip from the glass Belinda had given me, and nearly choked. It was not, as I had supposed, tea, but something a good deal stronger and unpleasant. I did not like spirits, but the subject had never come up.

I had not seen Belinda drink spirits before, and stared down at the cup in consternation before I found somewhere I could safely set it out of harm's way.

Then, as I rose to follow her down to the stage whether she wanted me to or not, Max reappeared at the edge of the stage and spoke, pitching his voice to be heard over the hubbub in the room below him.

"May I please have your attention." It was not a question, but a demand, and one that was obeyed. The room fell silent almost at once, even the musicians, having returned to their instruments after their short break, turning away from them again.

"We have at least one miscreant among us. He, or they, have taken something belonging to me. If it is returned to me now, there will be no consequences. If it is not, Sheriff Reilly will be holding the person or persons responsible in a manner the culprits will not appreciate."

The sheriff, his tall figure rising to Mr. Pepper's waist even though he stood below the stage, nodded firmly, then swung himself up to stand next to the little man. "I haven't had the need to give our jail an occupant since I've been here," he said in a clear firm voice reaching even to the back of the room, "but if the stolen property is not returned, and promptly, I will find whoever took Harry the pig and they will find out what incarceration is really like."

If I had thought the room was still when Mr. Pepper had begun to speak, the utter silence resulting from the sheriff's mention of the plaster pig felt as if the entire room had been stunned.

Not knowing what else to do, I made my way through the crowd to the stage. Mr. Pepper glanced down at me. "Miss Ogden? Do you know where Harry is?"

I shook my head. "What will happen now?"

He swallowed, his throat working, and said, "I don't know."

"I guess we'll find out," said Audrey, but she looked frightened. They all did. After the events earlier today, I supposed I could see why.

"Can anything be done?" I asked.

"We'll have to search," said Dan. "Let's get moving."

"No, wait," I said. They all stared at me. Even the crowd, which had begun to murmur and shift, as if heading for the doors at the far end of the room, stopped in their tracks.

"Why?" asked Max.

"I-I don't know." I only knew–

"Come on," said Rob. "Time's wastin', and that's the one thing we don't have right now."

And before I could say anything else, do anything else, to stop them, they were gone.

I do not mean they left the building. I mean they were gone. I could still hear the crowd, the multitude of footsteps pounding on the wooden floors, the voices organizing the search, the babble of the throng, the gradual lessening of the noise as the room – emptied. But I could no longer see them. It was like the first time I had entered the community hall, to hear voices from people who weren't there.

I stared down at myself, at my beautiful, shimmering pearl-colored gown. *I* still existed. I wondered if the townsfolk could see themselves or each other. If they could see me. If they still existed, or if everything that had happened to me in the last few months was a dream, caused by the cancer spreading to my brain. Was I still dying? I had never felt more alive in my life than I had since I came to Conconully.

My breathing echoed in the now-deserted room. The decorations hung forlornly from wall and ceiling, and the chairs seemed to lean almost drunkenly against the walls. A rustle came from behind the curtain. Was it a rat? I whirled to face it. Another rustle. No, not a rat. Were those footsteps? What would I see if I– I scrambled up onto the stage, no mean feat as it was raised several feet above the floor and I in a floor-length dress and dancing slippers.

But once there I found myself petrified with fear. Afraid to push that curtain aside. What could be back there? What would be back there?

It was then that I heard the voice, one I never thought to hear again. "Claudia?"

I swallowed. Tried to speak. Swallowed again. "Jean?"

CHAPTER 22

She sounded weak, and shaky, but I would have recognized that voice anywhere, even though months? a long time, at any rate, had passed since I'd last seen her, that day she'd put me on the train in Seattle, changing my life forever. I did not know why she was here, or how she'd made her own way here, or anything else. I simply knew I was glad she was still alive. *Not* dead. Glad? The word did not half describe how I felt right that moment.

"Come out. Where are you?"

The curtain moved aside, and I gasped. An old woman stood before me. Oh, the woman was Jean, no question about it. Her features, her height, her voice, all were the same. But all were altered, and everything else had changed. Her once-thick black hair, which she'd always kept in a daringly short bob, was now fine and white, her pink scalp visible through it. Her face creased with wrinkles as she smiled at me. Her figure stooped as if unable to carry even her slight weight.

"Have I changed so much, Claudia?"

Speechless, I stared for a moment, then stepped forward to wrap my arms around her. "Not so it matters," I murmured. After a long moment I pulled back, took her by her thin, veined hand, and led her to a chair.

"You must have questions," she told me.

I shook my head vehemently. "Not right now I don't. They told me you were *dead*. Do you know how much I've missed you?"

"I hope you didn't spend all of your time grieving me."

Wait. Had she *known*? Surely she hadn't *told* them to– No. I refused to believe it. I laughed in sheer relief. "I've made a good life. One I would not have had a chance at in the real world."

"So you are well?"

"Oh, yes. Doc Amy says I am completely cured."

This obviously pleased her; well, after all, it was why she'd sent me here, and I was grateful for it. But then she asked, "Doc Amy? What happened to Doc Stark?"

I hesitated, wondering precisely how much Jean knew about where she'd sent me. How she knew about Doc Stark. She seemed to know enough that I was not going to worry about censoring myself. Even if she did not know, she would not appreciate the effort. "He's gone. I think he faded away some time ago, before I arrived. Doc Amy was sent here – well, brought here – the same way I was. The same way Sheriff Reilly was. She's from the future, and so is he. So was I. It's 1893 here. Forever 1893. Or at least it was." I couldn't help wondering. "What year is it in the real world now?" It obviously wasn't 1910 anymore, judging from her aged appearance, in spite of the fact that I knew, even though I could not remember exactly, I hadn't been here more than a few months.

"1962."

1962? And what had she seen and done in fifty-two years without me? While I had thought she was *dead*. She's alive now, I thought. That's all that matters. I would ask her about her adventures later. For now I had other, more important questions. "How did you get here– no." She must have come with Oscar Miller. But if that was the case, then why hadn't she shown herself this afternoon out in the meadow? Was I the only one who could see her? The next question popped out of my mouth before she could answer the first one. "Have you seen Harry the pig?"

"Harry the–" she said, then made a strange wheezing sound. I made to thump her gently on the back, but she waved me away, and I realized suddenly she was laughing. Her merriment ended in a fit of coughing, and I fetched her a glass of, yes, that was tea, not strong spirits like what Belinda had handed me, from the refreshment table.

I tried to explain. "It's a plaster pig, or well, that's what it looks like, at any rate. It's-it's, oh, you're going to think I'm mad."

She took a sip, then a longer drink, and made to give me the glass. Her hand was shaking. The more I looked at her, the more I realized how fragile she was. I wondered if I was going to get the chance to ask her about her adventures. Or anything else.

I took the glass from her and set it on the floor beside my chair. "We need to get you to Doc Amy," I told her firmly.

"In a moment." She inhaled deeply, and her reedy voice strengthened. "To answer your question, yes, I know where the pig is. I did not realize it had a name."

"One of my pupils told me it was named after a local outlaw. Where is it?"

"So you're teaching again. I had hoped they'd take you on."

"It was why you sent me here in the first place, or so I thought." We were getting off the track. "Where is it?"

"I'm afraid it's gone."

"Yes, I know– you said you knew where!"

"I needed it, to get here."

Before I could ask how she knew to find it, or where to find it, or anything else, I heard a gasp behind me.

"Hello, Max," said Jean. "It's glad I am to be back again."

"Jean Clancy," said Max, "what on earth have you done?"

The little man was visible again. I don't know how he did it, or if he did it for the entire town or only himself and each of the townsfolk did it for themselves, or if it was something that simply happened, or precisely how or why or anything else, but I have never seen such consternation on anyone's face before or since.

"Max," said Jean, and coughed again. I handed her the tea, and she sipped some more, giving me a grateful glance, before she spoke again. "Max, you've been looking for a way out of this conundrum for a very long time. Since long before I left."

"I was glad you escaped, as you kept putting it. You were so all-fired determined to leave us."

"Not much use for a reporter in a place like Conconully," Jean said, as if that were explanation enough.

"So, Max," I said slowly, "you helped her, and then put it about that she'd died. Mauled by a bear, so I was told."

Jean remained silent, but I could see a guilty expression flit across her face before it was gone.

Max said, "I didn't know what would happen if it was known she'd left."

She raised an eyebrow, the sparse white hair barely visible. "Because others might want to go, too?"

"Yes." He bowed his head then raised it to look her straight in the eye. "And while you knew the odds, and were willing, others wouldn't."

"So you gave no one else a choice. I do wonder if you really did want this place to change."

"We have three new people now," the little man said defensively. "And she," he gestured at me, "saved young Brian Whittaker."

"The Millers are together now, too," I added. "Wherever they are."

At this, Jean smiled wistfully, which made me wonder if she knew where people went when they faded away, but she did not say anything.

Suddenly Max said, "And Alan Arngrim is dead."

Jean's head whipped up to stare at him. "Dead? Not faded?"

"Dead. Last New Year's. In an accident. And Daniel and Amy have married. So you see," he added after a moment, "things are changing here. And you can't have the good changes without the bad."

"Well," she said at last. "So perhaps that pig has served its purpose."

"No," said Max. "Not that much. Do you know what day it is?"

She shook her head. "Not here. When I drove from Seattle this morning," this morning, I thought in startlement. It's at least a two-day trip and she 'drove' it in little more than half a day? But she was still speaking. "It was October 15th."

"Well, it isn't October here," Max told her. "It's May 26th."

"I'd wondered— May 26th?"

"Yes. So now you see why Harry's disappearance is so damned important."

A breath drew in behind us. No, an enormous crowd of breaths, like the sigh of a breeze. When had all the townsfolk returned? And, if I turned around, would I see them?

But Jean did not look in the least perturbed. "Do you know what would happen if you didn't go through your little ritual every year?"

Max looked horrified, but he said, simply, "No."

"You never wanted to find out."

"I never wanted to watch everyone die." The gasp went up again. I suspected this was all as new to the townsfolk as it was to me.

Jean voiced my sentiments as exactly as I suspected she voiced those of the entire town. "You really do think you're God, don't you?"

"I don't– I never meant–"

"I think we all knew that, Max," said Rob. I glanced around, and, to my relief, he was not just a disembodied voice, but real and whole and standing there, with the rest of the town at his back. "If you ever felt like God because of this, it was because we let you."

Audrey, standing at his side, asked, "Don't you think we're as frightened as you are?"

But the little man had reclaimed his dignity. Somewhat. "I hadn't thought of it that way."

"We're every bit as responsible for the state of things here as you are," Rob said firmly.

"We all are," called out a voice from the back. Several others chimed in with similar sentiments.

"You-you know?" asked Max.

"Of course they do," said Amy. "Did you think you were running a puppet theater?"

"I guess I hadn't thought–"

"Not one of your more shining moments, Max," said Dan.

"No, no, I suppose not." He looked around the crowd, searching, rather helplessly, I thought, for something in all those faces. "But what do we do now?"

CHAPTER 23

"If I may make a suggestion," said Audrey at last. "Perhaps we ought to go on with the party."

"Without Harry?" Max's voice squeaked, and he cleared his throat.

"Without Harry," said Rob firmly. "If Miss– Clancy, is it still?" Receiving an amused nod from Jean, he went on, "If Miss Clancy is right, there's no purpose in searching for it. What will happen will happen. There's not much to be done about it now."

A sound like a teakettle on the boil came from Max's direction, and another wheezy laugh from Jean. "He's got you there," she told him. "You said you wanted change, but you keep insisting on doing things the same way over and over. When I come from, that's the definition of crazy."

Max spluttered again, but Dan was laughing, too. "Doing the same thing and expecting different results. Wasn't that Einstein?"

"I don't know," she told him comfortably. "Maybe."

People were already drawing away, into couples and groups. Conversations and the cheerful sounds of a party in progress began to pick back up. It was as if nothing had happened, and I marveled at them. The musicians had gone back to their corner, and Miss Grady struck up a tune on the piano. It was yet another song I did not recognize, but it sent Jean into another wheezing fit of laughter.

"Miss Clancy, if I may," Amy said, sounding concerned. She picked up Jean's wrist.

Jean tugged it away. "Don't you worry about me, young lady. I've had a good life, I'm where I want to be, and if Max is correct, it doesn't matter, anyway. Go dance with your fiancé. I don't think Max is right, but on the off chance the world is a crueler place than it should be, you'll want to be with your man, not wasting your time with an old woman like me." She waved her hands, and a pink-faced Amy let Dan draw her away, but not without more than one backward glance. How had she known?

"It's hard for her," Belinda said, coming to sit down beside us. "And it's going to be even harder for her and for Dan tomorrow."

Jean nodded, then said, "Would you introduce me to your friend, Claudia?"

"Jean, this is Miss Belinda Houseman, my–" and how was I to introduce the two people I loved most in the world to each other? I grasped Belinda's hand and brought it close to me, then let go. "My dearest friend here." And let it go. "Belinda, this is–"

But Belinda took Jean's thin, veined hand in both of hers. "You don't remember me, but I remember you, Jean Clancy. Men's trousers and tailored shirts and flat-heeled shoes. I had never seen a woman wearing the like before."

Jean was smiling now, but not in amusement. It was a gentle smile, one I had never seen on her face in the two years I'd known here back in Seattle. "I do remember you, Belinda. I am so glad to see you well." Her smile twisted a bit, more like the Jean I had known. "You haven't changed a bit."

The two women clasped hands, and I found I wasn't quite sure how I felt about it. Had they had a relationship like the one I had now with Belinda? I should have known. But Jean said, "You should see your face, Claudia. I'm not here to take Belinda from you."

"Indeed," Belinda added, "You could not. Nor Claudia from me."

"No," I said fervently, then felt guilty. And why should I? I shook my head. "I owe you much, Jean, but not this."

But Jean had slumped back in her chair, her head against the wall, her eyes closed. So suddenly still, her breast rising and falling under her plain gray blouse. She lifted a hand, the effort obvious. "Go on. It's been a long day, and I only want to listen."

I wanted to stay with her, but Belinda drew me to my feet. "She needs to rest. She's had a long day's travel. We'll send Doc Amy back to her by and by."

But even as I watched Jean, I didn't think Amy could do anything to help her. She seemed to be aging further by the moment, fading away the way Rose had. Without Harry, I could do nothing to stop it. As I stood there, Belinda's hand in mine, Jean grew more and more fragile before my eyes, paler and more transparent, until, at last, she simply wasn't there anymore.

"I suppose we should tell Max," Belinda said after a long moment. It felt wrong to do so somehow, although I knew I would not be able to articulate why.

"I suppose." But evidently Belinda felt the same way I did. The party had lost its luster, to understate the case beyond measure, and we made our way slowly and as unobtrusively as we could toward the back entrance, hoping, I think, to escape before anyone noticed.

But as we slipped out into the dark, warm, starry night, Rob and Audrey waited in the shadows outside the door. "She's gone?" he asked simply.

How had he known? "Yes," I told him.

He nodded. "Good night then."

Audrey echoed him, her normally cheerful face as solemn as I'd ever seen it.

We made our own way home, Belinda and I, in silence, hand in hand, the sounds of the party carrying on unabated, fading as we left it behind us.

I could not help wondering, as I fell asleep that night, what I would see out my window on the morrow.

But the morning broke clear and bright, as beautiful a day as could be imagined for a Sunday in May. Belinda's face wore a rather puzzled frown, as we ate breakfast and prepared for church, but she had little to say beyond a few absent pleasantries. As I was preoccupied myself, thinking about all that had happened the day before, I did not try to draw her out.

The townsfolk, every man, woman, and child, were making their way to the church as we left our house, but the air of confusion was almost palpable. Many carried umbrellas and wore galoshes in spite of the cloudless state of the sky, as if they expected a storm to sweep over the mountains and drench us at any moment. I had wondered at Belinda's insistence on bringing her waterproof and on me bringing mine. I carried it over my arm, in a rather incongruous contrast to my Sunday best dress and hat.

We walked side by side until we reached the church, and climbed the steps to enter it. People filed in all around us, and by the time the bell rang for the beginning of service, every pew was full and people were standing all around the walls. From comments I overheard as we waited, it sounded as if people who had not been to a church service in their entire lives were here this morning.

The bell rang a second time, and a third, but still the pulpit remained empty. The young man who led the choir stood next to it, looking as if he had no idea what to do without Max there to instruct him.

At last he raised his hands and the choir began to sing. They were halfway through the second verse of "When the Roll is Called Up Yonder" when the doors slammed closed at the back of the nave and Max hurried up the center aisle.

He looked as if he had not slept, no, as if he had not even gone home last night. He was still dressed in his top hat and tailcoat, the hat askew and his clothing rumpled enough to draw a whispered, "That man!" from Belinda, who I am quite sure was not pleased with his ill treatment of her hard work on his clothing.

He waved frantically, at first I supposed at the choir master, to get him to stop the music, but the man had his back to the congregation and it took a moment before even the choir noticed him. It was obvious when they had, though, because their voices trailed off, leaving Miss Grady at the piano to look up in confusion and stop as well. Only then did the choir master lower his arms and turn around.

"Max?" he said, sounding bewildered.

It was as if he had let loose a torrent.

"To the hills, everyone!" Max shouted. "Before the flood comes!"

A flood? All around me people were staring at him as if he'd lost his mind. I rather thought he had myself.

For a long moment, no one said anything. It was as if they were frozen, the way they had been in Brian's sickroom as Max and I watched them. It was so still, I could hear them breathing. As I hadn't in Brian's sickroom. I let out my own breath in relief. It was just shock, then, nothing more. Nothing inexplicable.

The moment began to drag out. Max stared around wildly, then said, desperately, "The flood. There has to be a flood." It was as if he thought if he said it with enough conviction, water would come flowing through the very building and sweep us all away.

Amy stood up, a slight form in a pale blue dress, and stepped out into the aisle. Slowly she walked toward Max, her hands held out in front of her. Dan followed her. I felt myself compelled to do the same, and I saw young Brian Whittaker squirming out past his sister and his father to join us as well.

"Max," said Amy, her voice soft and almost beseeching. "It's all right. There won't be a flood this year."

"There will be." Tears gleamed in the little man's eyes. "And this time it's going to be real. You're all going to die if you don't go to the hills." Determinedly, he strode past Amy, past Dan, past Brian who had come to stand next to me, up the steps to the pulpit. The tears were now streaming down his face, as he turned to face the congregation. "'I will lift up mine eyes to the hills, from whence cometh my help.' You must do more than lift your eyes. You must go there. Please."

I will say one thing for Maximilian Pepper. He could be almost unbelievably persuasive when he wanted to be, and he wanted nothing so much now as to get people out of what he thought was harm's way. Around us, the congregation felt it, too, and began to stir.

But the sheriff wasn't the sheriff for lack of authority, either. The four of us had followed Max to the pulpit, and now he pushed Max from it, none too gently. I don't think being gentle would have done the job.

He turned to the congregation. "There will be no flood this year, or, if we're lucky, any coming year. If there is, it will be the result of nature, not – magic, or will, or whatever this was, and if it happens, it will happen in its own time. We may have to run for the hills then, but not today." He lowered his voice until I could barely hear him, and added, "Not that we ever did before, either." He glared over at the choir master, who gazed helplessly back at him but then straightened and nodded decisively at Miss Grady.

She, in turn, shook herself and struck a chord on the piano. It rang out clear and pure, and the congregation stilled again. She played another, and another, and the opening bars of "Amazing Grace" began to take shape. Dan shook his head and, I thought in confusion, looked as if he wanted to laugh, but thankfully did not, and stepped down. The choir master took his place.

Amy took Max by the hand and walked him to the first, empty pew. She sat him down, then put herself next to him. Dan, then Brian, then I followed suit. The choir master took Miss Grady's cue, and began to sing. The choir in turn took his, and picked up the tune. All around me I heard the congregation begin to sing as well. And as the sunshine beamed in through the stained glass windows along the nave, the glorious, hopeful sound filled the little church, wrapping around us all.

EPILOGUE

The fall term had begun last week, and the woods around town were beginning to turn color – the huge maples with their leaves bigger than a dinner plate, their hues as vivid as the pumpkins in the field, and the larches with their pale delicate golden needles. The children were spilling out of the schoolhouse doors into the bright sunshine, shouting and laughing on this Friday afternoon. I must say I knew how they felt – I was very much looking forward to two days of peace and quiet before we started another week of learning. Not that I wouldn't be busy, what with creating new lesson plans and staying ahead of my older students. All of them kept me on my toes, and I was glad of it.

The flood Max had been so terrified of had never happened. Harry the pig had not reappeared, nor had Oscar Miller shown up with his wagon full of barrels. It worried some folks, I knew, including Belinda, whose stock of fabrics and notions was beginning to run low, and Rob, whose mysterious work in the garage at the south end of town apparently relied on bits and pieces hauled in from Omak to keep that odd truck of his running.

I cannot say it worried me, although I did wish for some more up-to-date schoolbooks. And new volumes for the library, which was no longer housed ad hoc in Doc Amy's parlor. The Conconully Library now occupied two of the former storerooms at the front of the community hall, and proudly displayed its wares in the hall's bay windows. It was very popular with the townsfolk, and donations of all sorts had been coming in at a fair clip. It was my joy and privilege to be in charge of it all, with help, and the transformation had neatly occupied my summer.

I spent most of my time there as well, when I was not at school. I had never thought I would enjoy the job of librarian, but as it turned out, it suited me far better than I would have expected. It also, Amy told me, suited me much better than it did her. And now that she and the sheriff were married, it was a good thing she had her parlor back.

I breathed the clean, dry mountain air with satisfaction. Nothing had changed with regard to my health, either, which also pleased the young doctor, almost as much as it did me. I would be forever grateful to Jean for sending me here, and, much as I missed her, knowing her fate meant a great deal to me. I was thankful to her for giving me that gift as well.

I was rounding the corner, headed home to Belinda and the supper I hoped Audrey had seen fit to send us in return for her new dress, when I heard the oddest sound.

It wasn't Rob's truck, which was not in operating condition at the moment, but it did sound very much like an internal combustion engine. One more like those I had been used to in Seattle, a very long time ago.

As I stood listening, people came outside, one by one at first, then in twos and threes and larger groups, all with their ears bent and their expressions curious. Belinda was one of the last to step out. I supposed her sewing machine had masked the racket.

"What on earth is that?" she asked me.

"It-it sounds like a horseless carriage." She stared at me, and I gazed back, helpless to say more.

Just then, the source of the commotion came roaring up over the hill, and the crowd surged forward, as if unable to stay behind.

It *was* a horseless carriage, almost like the ones I'd seen in Seattle a long time ago, but a vehicle for carrying freight rather than passengers. A logo was emblazoned on the side of the metal cab, a large M surrounded by an oval. The vehicle's open bed was contained by boards attached to metal rods at each corner. It was stacked full of barrels and crates.

I heard Belinda gasp beside me and I could not help letting my mouth stretch in a grin. I devoutly hoped at least some of those barrels were full of fabric and notions.

The machine jerked to a stop, and the engine died. The driver, a tall, blond, young man in a dusty white coat and a newsboy cap, jumped down. "I hope this is Conconully. Can someone tell me where I might find Max Pepper?"

But Max was pushing his way through the crowd, or, rather, the crowd was parting as if he were Moses and they were the Red Sea. "I'm Pepper."

The young man beamed at him. "Nice to meet you. I'm George Miller. My parents said to ask for you."

AFTERWORD

Thank you for reading *Reunion*. I hope you enjoyed it. Reviews help other readers find books. I appreciate all reviews, whether positive or negative.

If you're interested in reading more about the actual history behind the Tales of the Unearthly Northwest, please go to the Pathfinders pages on my website at http://mmjustus.com, where I have put together a bibliography of books and websites about the Okanogan Country and its history. The Photos pages there house a collection of snapshots of locations in these stories, along with one of Harry the pig.

Would you like to know when my next book is available? You can sign up for my new release email list at http://mmjustus.com, or follow me on Facebook at https://www.facebook.com/M.M.Justusauthor, or at Twitter @mmjustus.

Reunion is the second Tale of the Unearthly Northwest, following *Sojourn*. The third Tale, *Voyage*, will be available in 2016. In the meantime, you might also enjoy my Time in Yellowstone series, a set of historical novels (with just a little time travel) set mostly in and around Yellowstone National Park.

If you would like to read an excerpt from the first Time in Yellowstone novel, *Repeating History*, please turn the page.

IT WAS JUST A GEYSER

In 1959, 20-year-old college dropout Chuck McManis strolls the geyser boardwalks in Yellowstone National Park when an earthquake plunges him eighty years back in time, into the middle of an Indian war. Into his personal past, too – his great-grandfather, his boyhood idol, but not a hero after all.

Hapless Chuck needs instructions for sheer survival. He will not abandon Eliza Byrne, the woman who teaches him. But nothing matters if they never make it back to civilization. No matter when it could be.

CHAPTER 1

August 15, 1959

My summer school grades arrived the day after Granddad's funeral. I didn't bother opening them. I knew what was inside. Granddad would have appreciated the irony. I knew Dad wouldn't, and I was glad I'd got to the mail first. Dad was broken up enough over Granddad's death as it was. Although with him it wasn't easy to tell.

"It's time to go." He looked, as usual, like the accountant he is. Bland and smooth in his gray suit, white button-down shirt, and navy blue tie.

"Sure." I wasn't wearing a suit, just jeans and a plaid shirt and my motorcycle boots. I didn't pat the pocket I'd stuffed the envelope in. Didn't want to draw attention to it. I pushed my glasses up and ran a hand over my dishwater blond buzz cut instead. Then tugged the sleeves of my leather jacket back down over my wrists. The curse of being a beanpole.

He looked me up and down and frowned but didn't say anything else as he locked the door behind us and led the way to his car. At least not until I went to my bike instead.

"You're not riding that *thing* to the lawyer's office."

I swung my leg over the Harley. "Sure I am."

"No, you're -" The rest of the rant, which I knew by heart, was lost in the rumble of the bike's engine. Music to my ears.

* * *

"And that's the last of it," Mr. Pritchard said, handing me Granddad's pocketwatch. So there had been something in the will for me, after all, as familiar as if I'd known it all my life. Which I had. I closed my hand around the smooth metal case, then stuffed it deep into the bottom of my jeans pocket. That was one thing I never wanted to lose. The lawyer straightened the sheaf of paper he was holding, and looked at Dad. I leaned back in my chair and stared out the window overlooking the street, wishing for a hamburger. Lunch had been a long time ago.

"I don't understand why he was so adamant about getting in here to see you two weeks ago," Dad said. "Nothing appears to have changed from the version he gave me last year."

Mr. Pritchard looked apologetic. "I should have said almost the last of it. The codicil he had me add at our last meeting doesn't have anything to do with the disposition of his property, but of his and your mother's remains."

That was creepy. Cremation was even worse than getting buried.

"I've bought a niche for both of them out at Cherry Hills," Dad said in that tone he has. *This is the way it is, period.*

Cherry Hills was the last place my grandparents would have wanted to end up, not that they were going to be able to tell the difference now. It's the ritziest cemetery in Denver, all carefully mowed lawns and fancy statuary. Besides, neither one of them liked Denver to begin with. Granddad had only given up and moved here to be closer to the Dad and me after Grandmother died and his health went downhill.

And when Dad had insisted. Granddad hadn't put up nearly as much of a fight about it as I'd thought he would, though.

"He was very specific about what he wanted done," Mr. Pritchard said, with almost exactly the same tone..

"Well, what *does*-" Dad broke off. I could almost see the blood draining from his face. *Why?* It couldn't be that bad. There's only so much you can do with a pile of ashes, after all. "No. Absolutely not."

Mr. Pritchard looked kind of surprised. "But I haven't even told you what he wanted done yet." Then he turned to me.

I could have sworn they'd completely forgotten I was there. God knows I was wishing I wasn't. What I wanted was to get on my bike and ride far away from this office, from Denver, from my grades burning a hole in my pocket, from the fact that Granddad was dead...

"Your grandfather wished for you to take their ashes back to Yellowstone and scatter them there. He wanted them left where he and your grandmother spent so much of their lives and were so happy together. I've arranged permission from the park service, and made reservations for you at the Old Faithful Inn for three nights starting tomorrow."

All I could think was *oh, my God. Really? Yes! Thank you thank you thank you, Granddad.* He couldn't have given me anything better if he'd tried. I sobered. Except to stay alive.

Mr. Pritchard paused, watching, smiling slightly at me. I could see Dad out of the corner of my eye, all the blood back in his face turning it red with – why was he so mad? Yeah, he didn't get it, wouldn't get it, but it wasn't that big a deal. Just four lousy days. In Yellowstone. Where I'd spent the best times with Grandmother and Granddad, growing up. A chance to get the hell out of here. "You should have plenty of time. If I understand correctly, you won't be going back to college this fall."

My jaw dropped, but before I could say anything, Dad took a deep breath. "And why not?" His fists were clenched on the arm of the chair, and he was past just red. He looked like he was going to explode. "What did you do this time, and why the *hell* didn't you tell me before it went this far?"

"I, uh." My tongue stuck in my throat. *Well, at least he knows now.* "I, uh, flunked Business Law. And Economic Analysis."

"*Again?*" He looked like he wanted to strangle me. I guess the only reason he didn't was where we were.

Mr. Pritchard was looking apologetic again. "I'm sorry. I thought you knew. I spoke out of turn."

I turned on him. Anything so I didn't have to look at Dad. "How the-How did you know about my grades? I just got them today."

His smile this time was almost a smirk. "Perhaps the two of you need to go home and talk this over."

Over my dead body. Which is what it was likely to be by the time Dad got done with me.

Dad apparently had the same idea, because he stood and grabbed me by the arm. I'm taller than he is, but he's got a helluva grip for a 62-year-old man. "Come on, son."

I glanced back at Mr. Pritchard as Dad dragged me out of the room. *Thanks a lot, Mister.*

* * *

I'm twenty years old. It's not like my father can stick me in my room and expect me to stay there. I packed up my duffel bag and snuck out that night while Dad was on the phone, talking to God knows who about God knows what. Well, not God knows what, although what Dad thought he could do to get Colorado State University to take me back again was sort of beyond me.

I spent what was left of the night at a diner, dozing with my coffee going cold on the table in front of me, and arrived at Pritchard's office at the crack of dawn the next morning. He got there pretty darned early himself, and he didn't seem to be surprised to see me. He handed me an envelope full of cash, gave me the paperwork for permission to pick up the ashes and the directions to the crematorium, which was one seriously strange place, and wished me good luck.

I was on the road to Yellowstone, duffel bag on the back of my bike, before rush hour even got started.

* * *

It was full dark and my legs were aching like a son of a gun by the time I came over the last rise to Old Faithful. I was so tired I was about to fall off the bike. But I'd made it.

Lights illuminated the valley below. The Inn, a huge pile of logs with windows, was surrounded by smaller buildings that made it look like the thing had had puppies, the river flowing between plumes of steam.

The road curved around past the low slung lodge and its cabins, past the visitor center, to the porte cochere, which had once protected fancy guests a long time ago, and now stood guard over people in jeans and pedal pushers towing their own suitcases.

I found a place to park the bike, and unhooked my duffle with one hand while swiping the road dust off my face with the other.

"Ooh," voices rose around me. "It's erupting."

I turned to watch with everyone else. I've seen Old Faithful go off dozens of times, but it had been a long time since Grandmother died, Granddad retired and I went off to college. I let my duffle drop to the ground and grinned. I could hear the roar over the people around me, through the memories in my head.

Dammit, I'd missed this place.

The geyser spent itself in a few minutes, and I watched, tickled, as people applauded. They always did, like the geyser was alive. Then, the show over, I picked up my bag and headed inside to claim my room.

* * *

I didn't bother with the Inn's dining room. Too pricey and too fancy. The store a few hundred yards away had a soda fountain. One of Granddad's and my favorite treats when Grandmother had gone to Jackson or West to go shopping for the day had been greasy hamburgers and fries at that fountain.

It was at the back of the store, a row of little round red stools and a metal counter, with a bunch of shiny chrome restaurant equipment and a pass-through behind it. As I approached it looked deserted. I hoped it wasn't closed. The rest of the store was busy with tourists buying souvenirs, but it was after the normal time most people ate supper.

Then, as I sat down on one of the stools, I saw this cute little rear end, round and sweet in a red and white striped skirt, bent over behind the counter.

"Hi," I said, and she shot up, straws spraying out of the box in her hand as she squeezed it.

"Oh! You startled me." She seemed to realize what she was doing to the box, and dropped it on the counter. Straws slithered everywhere, and she and I both made grabs for them.

Her front view was as good as the back. Nicely stacked, pretty face, brown curly hair escaping from a net.

She caught my eye, then fumbled for an order pad. "What can I get for you?"

I smiled at her. She smiled back. *Good.* "A hamburger, please. Fries. A Coke."

She scribbled it down. "It'll be just a minute." She turned to stick the order on the spindle in the pass-through window, and called out, "Joe! Order!"

Joe turned out to be Jo, a middle-aged woman wearing an apron shiny with grease who filled out her red-and-white dress a lot more solidly than my waitress did. She scowled at the order slip. "Grill's supposed to be closing."

"I know, Jo, but-"

"Yeah, you're a soft touch for a cute guy."

I smiled at her. The scowl melted from her eyes, although she tried to keep it on her mouth, and she slapped a burger on the griddle. I could hear it sizzle.

"Thanks, ma'am," I told her. "I've been on the road since six a.m."

"Yeah, yeah." Her gaze shot to the other end of the counter. "Loverboy at two o'clock."

The girl and I both turned to look. Her gaze fell, and she went back to picking up straws.

"Hey, Alice, what's a guy got to do to get some service around here?"

So much for my idea to ask her if she'd like to go for a beer later.

The guy was almost as tall as I am, and I'm six foot two, but he was a lot broader, and it looked like mostly muscle. He scowled at me. I shrugged and shoved my glasses up my nose. She'd been fair game till he showed up, but I wasn't going to muscle in on him now.

Reluctantly, as if pulled by strings, Alice made her way to the other end of the counter. As soon as she got within arm's length, he reached out and snagged her by the elbow, tugging her around the end of the counter so she practically bounced off of him. She sent an apologetic glance back towards Jo, who waved her off.

I sighed, and Jo turned towards me.

"Know anyplace a guy can get a beer around here?" I asked her. She smirked at me.

"Only place in the village licensed to sell liquor is the bar in the Inn, and they don't sell to underaged."

I ignored the dig since I was used to that kind of thing, swallowed my last French fry, and paid her.

Beer at the Inn would probably cost an arm and a leg, but what the hell. It had been one long day. There was enough money in Pritchard's envelope, and I'd earned it.

* * *

When I woke up it was pitch black and freezing. I was in my room, sprawled on top of the covers, with my head at the foot of the bed. I still had all my clothes on, which was a good thing or I probably would have frozen to death. I still had my boots on, as I discovered when one of them clunked against the log headboard. The vibration made my head rattle. I couldn't remember how I'd gotten there, but I must have managed it under my own steam. Nobody here I knew to do it for me. I sat up, and immediately decided the last couple of beers had been a mistake. My head rang, the room spun, and oh, man, I had to piss. Bigtime. Good thing the sink was handy, since the toilet was down the hall.

When I was done, I plunked myself back down on the bed and realized I wasn't going to get back to sleep anytime soon. The radiator was hissing, which didn't explain why I was freezing my ass off. Something was ruffling the curtains. I went over to look and discovered the window was open. That explained the temperature, at any rate. I closed it, and stayed to stare out into the night. The moon was full, shining off the river in the distance, illuminating the boardwalks and the trees, the occasional plume of steam. Not a soul to be seen. I pulled out Granddad's pocketwatch. Past eleven. Why not?

I hoisted my duffel onto the bed. The box was at the very bottom, tucked into one end where it had settled. I pried at the plastic lid with a fingernail. It refused to open. I sat for a minute, staring at it. Knife. I stood and began rooting through my pockets. That turned up nothing besides the watch but my room key and an unwrapped breath mint, growing a nice case of pocket crud. I brushed it off and stuck it in my mouth to get rid of it. Bad move. If I thought my mouth had tasted scuzzy before, it was twice as nasty now.

After I spit the mint into the garbage can, I found my pocketknife in the toe of my spare shoes, strangely enough. Gingerly I slid the blade along the seam of the box. With no warning, the lid snapped open and a poof of dust rose, straight into my face.

I snapped the lid back down, cussing. It wouldn't stay. "Okay. Okay." I set the box down on the little table next to the bed and backed away from it, swiping at my face, hoping I wasn't inhaling Grandmother and Granddad. Once the dust settled, I approached it again, and carefully closed the lid, feeling for the catch and pressing hard. This time it stayed. I let my breath out in a long whoosh.

I picked my pocketknife up off the floor, grabbed my leather jacket and the box, and headed out the door.

* * *

It was even colder outside, too cold for August even up here. And eerie, with no one around. I could hear sounds coming from the lodge across the road, music, thumps, and somebody's muffled laughter. They seemed very far away.

My momentum got me as far as the beginning of the boardwalk, where my boots sounded like somebody banging on a door out there in the middle of the night. I tried to straighten out my steps, but I guess I was still more toasted than I'd thought I was. No railings to lean on, either. I could have used one just then.

The bridge over the river echoed, too, but the water rushing underneath drowned some of that out. And it had railings. I stopped and watched the current for a while, leaning on the railing, but not too hard. I didn't want to topple over into the river, which seemed way too possible right then. Too much beer. *Sorry, Granddad.*

I took a better hold on the box. Time to move on. Granddad's will hadn't been all that specific about where to scatter the ashes, as long as it was in the park. I stopped and tried to think about it. Around Old Faithful seemed like kind of a cliché, and, anyway, I couldn't get close enough to the geyser anymore to scatter them properly. Not like when I was a kid and the only thing keeping a person from striding up and peering down the hole was his own good sense. Or his Granddad the park ranger. Besides, I was already on the other side of the river.

Observation Point seemed like a good idea until I started up the hill, grasping at tree branches and tripping over rocks in the dark. But I was halfway up before that dawned on me, and by then it was a matter of principle. So I kept going, and eventually I stood at the top, overlooking the whole valley in the moonlight.

The quiet was almost too much. No breeze, no sounds of animals – *they're all asleep, you idiot, everything with any sense is sound asleep* – no, wait a minute. I could hear splashing, muted by distance, and sank down on a rock to watch Old Faithful go off, as if it had waited for me to take my seat. I stared at it, spellbound, as if it was the first time I'd ever seen it. It certainly was the first time I'd ever had it all to myself, water spraying in the moonlight, steam clouds lifting into the sky.

Too soon, it was finished, and the night sounds took over again. A breeze picked up in the trees, and something chittered, then fell silent again. The scene below me looked like a painting. I felt like one of the early explorers, watching something no one would believe existed. The half-dozen remaining lighted windows of the inn might have been stars, the distant fires in the campground on the other side of the lodge might have belonged to an early expedition, or to old Colter himself. Or to the Indians. I shivered.

Here you are. Get it over with and get back to bed. I fished my pocketknife out and pried at the lid.

The box opened easily this time, and the dust wafted away into nothing in the slight breeze, more quickly than I expected. I shook out the last few bits. "Hope this does it for you, Granddad," I said into the night. "Miss you. Grandmother, too." I did. They were my real parents, the ones who'd taken me in and raised me after my mother died when I was born and Dad couldn't handle the whole situation. They were the ones who'd taught me who I was and who I wanted to be, who'd given me everything. Who'd understood me.

I didn't cry then. I don't cry much, at least not on the outside. But my chest was tight and my eyes burned, even though I knew I was doing the right thing. This trip felt like one last present they'd given me. Suddenly I was very glad things had worked out this way. In spite of having to sneak out on Dad. "You're home," I told them. "So am I. Thanks. I'll come back some day. I promise."

I tucked the box back under my arm and headed down the hill.

It was a fine night. Yeah, it was freezing, but my leather jacket kept me warm. The stars were shining like high beams against the sky and the beer was finally wearing off and I felt good about what I'd done. Sad, but good. I couldn't quite bring myself to go back inside. Not yet. To go back inside was to say the whole thing was over. I had three nights, so I didn't have to go back and face my real life yet – *this is real life, dammit.* Flunking out of college was what felt like a dream right now. Or a nightmare. So I didn't go in. I got myself down the trail to the valley, and decided to take a little stroll instead. It wasn't likely I'd ever have the place to myself like this again, unless I got drunk for the next two nights, which didn't feel like a bad idea now that the hangover was wearing off.

I'd wandered a ways down the path when the ground began to vibrate under my feet.

I looked up from my thoughts to find myself in front of Grand Geyser. I grinned. The tremors meant I might get to watch another eruption before I went back in. I sat down crosslegged on the planks to wait and watch.

The moon gleamed on the pool under the boardwalk, the ripples growing into small waves as the vibrations magnified. A splash, another splash, this one bigger than the first, a chugging racket that sounded like the propellers on an airplane about to take off...

The earthquake, it had to be an earthquake, hit like a giant pounding a sledgehammer. The boardwalk – bounced. With me on it. It was like riding a bucking bronco. I grabbed the edge of the boards, and hung on. Grand's pool was churning like a crazy thing now. Water hit me on the back, the heat soaking through my jacket and shirt.

Then it all stopped. "That was a helluva ride," I said into the suddenly still darkness, the moon glimmering off the still sloshing pool. My thumb hurt. I held it up a few inches from my nose. A splinter was lodged under the nail. I grasped it between my teeth and yanked it out. Tugged the tail of my shirt out to stanch the blood. And stared around.

Everything seemed to be holding its breath. Not a bit of movement, except the water draining under my feet. Not a sound, except for the now-fading hiss of the runoff. I took a deep breath and started to get up.

That's when the big one hit.

Available from all major retailers.

About the Author

M.M. Justus spent most of her childhood summers in the back seat of a car, traveling with her parents to almost every national park west of the Mississippi and a great many places in between.

She holds degrees in British and American literature and history and library science, and a certificate in museum studies. In her other life, she's held jobs as far flung as hog farm bookkeeper, music school secretary, professional dilettante (aka reference librarian), and museum curator, all of which are fair fodder for her fiction.

Her other interests include quilting, gardening, meteorology, and the travel bug she inherited from her father. She lives on the rainy side of the Cascade mountains in Washington state, within easy reach of all of its mysterious places.

Please visit her website and blog at http://mmjustus.com, on Facebook at https://www.facebook.com/M.M.Justusauthor, and on Twitter @mmjustus.

BOOKS BY M.M. JUSTUS

TALES OF THE
UNEARTHLY NORTHWEST
Sojourn
"New Year's Eve in Conconully"
Reunion

TIME IN YELLOWSTONE

Repeating History
True Gold
"Homesick"
Finding Home

Much Ado in Montana

*Cross-Country: Adventures Alone Across
America and Back*

Made in the USA
Columbia, SC
15 November 2017